LOVE ME AT
Sunset

LOVE ME AT
Sunset

A Romano Family romance

Lucinda Whitney

Lange House Press

Edited by Michele Holmes and Haley Swan
Cover design ©2018 Lange House Press
Layout and Formatting by LJP Creative
Published by Lange House Press

First Printing October 2017

ISBN 13: 978-1-944137-26-7
ISBN 10: 1-944137-26-2

Nem que outras coisas mudem, começamos
e acabamos com família.

Other things may change, but we start
and end with family.

Romano Family

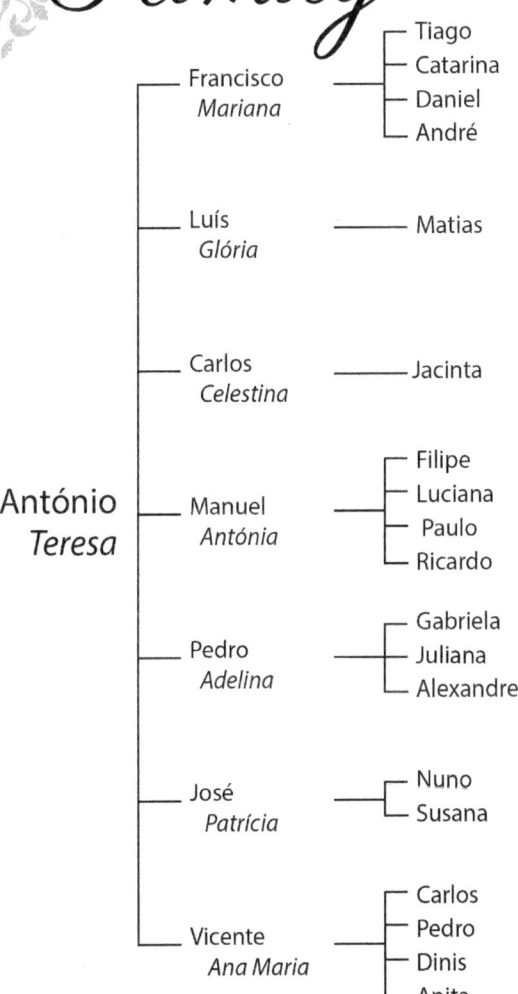

António
Teresa

- **Francisco** / *Mariana*
  - Tiago
  - Catarina
  - Daniel
  - André
- **Luís** / *Glória*
  - Matias
- **Carlos** / *Celestina*
  - Jacinta
- **Manuel** / *Antónia*
  - Filipe
  - Luciana
  - Paulo
  - Ricardo
- **Pedro** / *Adelina*
  - Gabriela
  - Juliana
  - Alexandre
- **José** / *Patrícia*
  - Nuno
  - Susana
- **Vicente** / *Ana Maria*
  - Carlos
  - Pedro
  - Dinis
  - Anita

CHAPTER ONE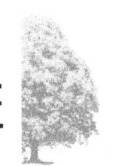

*H*ow much hope could a place hold for a new beginning?

Afonso arrived at the stone wall and dropped the canvas bag on the side of the road. The intricate monogram on each panel of the iron gate confirmed he was at the right place. Casa do Sol Poente— Sunset Manor. Was this his fresh start? A place named after his favorite time of day could only bring good luck.

In the valley below, the first shadows cast by the setting sun already inched closer to the foothills of the small village of Sete Fontes. The view opened far beyond the winding river to the red-roofed houses dotting the hills on the other bank.

He reached for his water bottle and took a long swig, appreciating the differences in the air around him. No traffic noises. No congested streets and crowded sidewalks. And more notably, no sounds of churning industrial-sized washers, the hiss of steam irons, and the always-present loud-cursing men he'd had to put up with during laundry duty.

Only the languorous clangs of the church bell and a couple of dogs barking at each other on a farm down the hill.

A slow smile pulled at the corners of his mouth. He liked it already.

The walk from the village had taken close to an hour, and he hadn't passed any other houses or farms in the last fifteen minutes. The promise of solitude bloomed more real than he'd thought possible.

Afonso swung the bag over his shoulder and placed the empty bottle in an outside pocket. The gate was ajar, and he passed through easily, noting the signs of neglect. The original color was hard to pick amid the rust stains, and it could use a good cleaning and a new coat of paint.

As he climbed the winding road past the bend, rows of hydrangea bushes lined the lichen-covered walls, the large blue petals brightening the old stones. Through the branches, a peek of stone caught Afonso's attention, but the thick foliage hid the rest of the house from view.

After the paved road curved sharply in the other direction, Afonso stopped. A woman stood at the edge of a weed-infested path, facing a row of mature linden trees. The golden light outlined her delicate figure, contrasting with the wildness of the bushes and vegetation behind her, a mass of twisted greens of various shades speckled with tiny buds of the red, pink, and yellow of a once-grand rose garden.

Before he had the chance to make his presence known, the woman clutched her middle and doubled over, retching violently.

Afonso turned away from her and took a step back, torn between the urge to help her and the need to give her privacy. Had she eaten something bad, or was she ill? His former training kicked in and his mind went through a list of possibilities.

After a few moments, she straightened and wiped her mouth with the back of her hand. She mumbled something and shook her head, the disgust in her tone clear and unmistakable.

Afonso shifted his bag. "Hey, are you okay?"

The woman shrieked and jumped back with a hand over her chest. When she turned to face him, her eyes widened with surprise, which was quickly replaced with something stronger. "This is private property," she yelled. "Who are you, and what are you doing here?" She flicked her eyes to the ground and her cheeks flamed red. "Are you some kind of pervert spying on people?"

Afonso shouldered his bag behind his back and raised his hands in a show of conciliation. "I'm sorry if I caught you at a bad moment. I promise I'm not spying on you." He spoke slowly, trying to diffuse the tension. "I'm here to meet with the owner."

She crossed her arms over her middle, and this time the disgust in her expression was surely directed at him. "He should be in the main house." Her tone was curt.

Afonso stepped back onto the private driveway and nodded a quick thanks to her.

Her eyes narrowed at him as she watched him go by. "You better not be lying."

He paused and met her eyes. "I don't lie." All the lies were in the past. He was done with that life.

She didn't reply, but her left eyebrow raised. In contradiction or skepticism, he couldn't tell.

When Afonso reached the clearing, he looked back, but she was gone. He gave himself a mental shake to push the strange encounter from his mind.

The manor house was large and almost as imposing as he'd expected. Its neoclassical style was reflected in the symmetric lines of the windows on the ground floor and the row of Juliet balconies on the first floor. From the red-tiled roof, a pair of attic dormers rose on each side. A wide staircase led to the front where a heavy, paneled wooden door matched the green of the painted shutters. The effect was almost striking, minimized only by the intense disarray of all the vegetation surrounding the area. In its glory days, the granite house's grandeur must have been impressive.

Afonso climbed the steps. Even the door knocker was a classic. He lifted the iron hand holding a ball and smacked it against the metal plate on the wood surface.

After a new knocks, the door swung open.

A dark-haired man in his midthirties stood at the entrance. "Hello. Can I help you?" His tone was friendly.

"I'm looking for Filipe Romano," Afonso said.

The man extended his hand. "I'm Filipe Romano." His grip was strong, and he made eye contact. "Are you Afonso Cortez by any chance?"

Afonso nodded. "I am."

Filipe Romano's expression relaxed into a smile. "Praise the heavens. I thought you'd changed your mind about coming. Please, come in."

The faint scent of new construction and aged wood permeated the air. The area was clean and void of furniture but for a large rug covering the aged marble floor in front of the stairs and a free-standing coat-rack made of heavy wood. The main staircase split in two at the first landing, one to each side of the house. The oval skylight let the sunshine in to spill naturally down the staircase, casting shadows into the corners.

Afonso took a moment to study Filipe Romano. He looked like a slightly older version of his cousin Matias, Afonso's former boss. The family resemblance was evident in the same brown eyes and high fore-head. "Sorry I'm late. The walk up was a bit longer than I thought."

"You walked from the village?"

"I'm without my own transportation at the moment." He was without a lot of things, a car being the least of those.

5

Filipe brought a hand to his chin as he gave Afonso an appraising look. "Well, I'm glad you made it." He gestured to the floor by the door. "Just leave your things there. I'll show you later where you can put them." He turned down the hallway to his right, and Afonso followed him to the first room.

"This is the music room. Well, it's an empty room now, but that's what the original design called for and I tried to preserve that."

In the corner, under a cover, the skeleton of a grand piano stood silent. Afonso turned away from it and flexed this fingers involuntarily.

Filipe glanced in the same direction. "That old piano came with the house, and I still don't know what to do it."

Afonso pretended he didn't either.

"I'm nearly done with the interior remodel." Filipe kept walking and gestured at the door opening as they passed from one room to the next without the connection of a hallway. "The kitchen and bathrooms are all done, and the interiors have all been painted. I'm trying to decide what to do about the decorating."

"Impressive work," Afonso said. The wood floors looked original as well, having been refinished to a polished gloss.

Filipe pushed the last door, and they entered a room that looked half-lived-in. A heavy mahogany desk sat by one of the windows, and a pair of wing-back chairs and a sofa in dark leather were positioned in front of the fireplace. The wall opposite the windows was lined with floor-to-ceiling shelves in the same mahogany, conspicuously void of books. From what he'd seen so far, even without furniture and decoration the mansion was grand.

"The books are in storage, and I didn't have the time to unpack them yet." Filipe gestured around. "So this is the office and library. In case you're wondering, the built-in shelves are original, but I had the desk made to match. Not exactly my taste but it goes with the house." He walked to the desk and cleared a pile of papers to the side. "The house sits square with the cardinal points and we still call this side the west wing." He unfurled a blueprint, tucked the corners under books, and set a solid glass paperweight on the surface.

Afonso approached and listened to Filipe's explanations of the house.

"For the time being, you'll be working in the areas immediately surrounding the house." Filipe tapped the paper again. "The road from the gate to the front door needs to be cleared. And the formal gardens require a lot of attention." He brought a smaller map from under the blue print. "These are the original plans that I was able to unearth in Castelo Branco's register. There's an English-type garden with roses and boxwood edges." He paused and looked up to Afonso. "You do have experience with yard work, don't you?"

"I have hands-on experience, but no formal training." All the summers Afonso had spent at his grandparents' working on the farm might finally pay off.

"That's good enough for me." Filipe turned back to the map, and Afonso followed along a series of geometric designs with numbers and a key written in a curled script on the margin.

Filipe slid a drawer open and drew out a tablet. "I hired a landscape designer who outlined each stage of the cleaning and restoration that needs to happen before the new plants come in." He pushed the tablet into Afonso's hands, and Afonso swiped the screen as he looked through the color-coded plans. "For now, I decided to start clearing the overgrowth and moving on with some of the smaller projects. It's all there on the tablet. Of course, you can always call me or send me a text if you have any questions," Filipe said.

Afonso raised his head from the screen. He must have missed something. Why would he need to call Filipe? "Won't you be here every day?"

Filipe sat on the sofa and indicated the chair to Afonso. "My plans changed. I'm in the middle of acquiring a property by the coast, and I need to be there. As much as I'd like to supervise the garden's restoration, it's not as pressing as the other project is. That's why I need a person I can trust to stay here."

Afonso returned the tablet to Filipe. "You do know where I've just come from, don't you?" What exactly had Matias Romano told his cousin about Afonso? As much as Afonso wanted this job, if Filipe wasn't aware of his past, he would quickly take back his offer.

"If you're referring to your recent release from prison, yes, I am aware of that." He leaned back and crossed an ankle over his knee. "Even though I haven't seen my cousin in a while, we stay in touch. Matias knew I needed someone to take over the grounds keeping, and he recommended you. I don't know you, but I trust my cousin, and that's enough for me." He paused. "We all make mistakes. It's how we learn from them and move forward that proves our integrity. Do you still want the job?"

Afonso appreciated that Filipe was direct. "Yes, I do," he said slowly, trying to tamper his eagerness. Afonso wanted this job more than he remembered wanting anything in his recent life. He would do his best to make sure he was worthy of that trust.

Filipe spent the next half hour going over a detailed list of each clearing stage, taking the time to answer all of Afonso's questions about the house and the property. He pulled out two sets of key rings. "This one has the keys to vehicles, including the one to the truck. You'll need to get supplies from town and haul equipment around the property. This ring has the keys to the house, the detached garage, and the outbuildings. There's a small house to the east side where the caretakers live. They pretty much came with the property when I bought it, and I didn't have the heart to kick them out. I restored their house and renewed their contract even though they're getting on with years and I'd rather they retire." He glanced at his watch. "I was going to introduce you, but I think they left already. The Silvas are only here between Monday mornings and Friday afternoons, as they spend the weekends at their home in the village. Sometimes they have family who comes by, and then they drive down together."

Afonso nodded, adding another mental note to his list.

After all the instructions, including the location of the Wi-Fi tower and login information, Filipe presented two copies of a simple contract, which they both signed. Five months—from the last of May to the end of October—with an option to renew, if both parties agreed.

He handed Afonso a credit card. "All the expenses associated with the house and property are on this card. You don't have to worry about bookkeeping. I got someone for that."

Afonso resolved to keep all the receipts just in case.

"There's one more thing." Filipe paused and rubbed his chin. "I have a relative staying in the west wing." He indicated the area above them. "She's been here for a few weeks, and she's staying for as long as she wants or needs to." He reached for his wallet and drew out another card. "Anything she needs goes on this card."

Afonso hesitated. "Wouldn't it be better if she keeps the card herself?"

"She has a card of her own, but she's quite stubborn and doesn't drive. I usually take her lists when I go shopping as well. Just make sure she's got what she needs." After a pause, he added, "She was recently widowed and hasn't been ready to socialize much."

At first, Afonso thought of the woman in the old rose garden, but she was far too young to be widowed. His experience with older people was limited to the interactions he'd had with the ship's passengers, but he had observed plenty of stubbornness in that age range.

He took the card from Filipe. "I'll keep the receipts and send you digital copies."

Filipe looked at him. "Sure, that works. She's resting or I'd introduce you. Actually, it might be best to give her a wide berth until she's feeling better. Grieving has taken a toll on her, and she's been quite sick."

"Yes, of course."

"And she might need some rides to Castelo Branco, but you can hire somebody for that if you're too busy."

Afonso nodded, not knowing what to say until he knew the old lady better. "Do you have problems with villagers coming on the grounds?"

Filipe blew out a long breath. "It hasn't been a problem, since the house is a bit of stretch from the village. Just be firm, but kind, if you see anyone around who's not supposed to be here."

Afonso frowned. The mysterious woman must be a relative of the caretakers, visiting them for a few days. He was not looking forward to another confrontation with her. Hopefully they wouldn't cross paths again.

Catarina leaned back against the stuffed chair in Filipe's bedroom as she watched him pack. "Say that again, please? I don't think I heard you right." Her mouth pressed into a hard line.

Filipe chuckled. "Don't start pouting, Catarina. That doesn't work on me. Besides, you knew I was looking for someone to take over the grounds before I leave." He shoved a few items of clothing into a day bag. "I should have hired someone two months ago."

She crossed her arms over her chest. "Do you really have to leave? I won't have anyone to talk to."

"Why didn't you call your mom like I suggested? Or one of your brothers? Or even a friend?"

She shook her head. "It's still too soon for that. I wouldn't want the media rags to get a clue on my maiden name." She hadn't used the Romano name in over six years. She was hiding in the district of Castelo Branco, hours away from Lisbon and from everything that had been her former life, hopefully far enough that no one would recognize her. Staying inside the property ensured nobody would. And even though Filipe was a high-profile business man, well known throughout the country, he'd never announced the purchase of the manor house. The remodel had been slow going as well, not attracting any attention beyond the few villages around the area. Any kind of attention was the last thing she wanted at this point in her life.

Filipe pulled the zipper closed. "You can always come with me."

"I can't." The less she was out and about the better, and the coast was more populated than this area.

"It's your choice, but I'll be away for a few weeks at least. The new guy I hired can get you anything you need, but you'll have to talk to him." He smoothed the traditional bedspread on the bed, then hoisted his bag. "I should have introduced you two before he left to the village."

"You hired him already? Did you even run a background check on him?"

"Yes, he's hired. Got the contract signed, the financial paperwork filled out, and he'll be around for at least five months." Filipe paused and looked pointedly at her. "And I did run a background check even though he was personally recommended by Matias."

Catarina wrinkled her forehead. "Matias who?"

Filipe arched an eyebrow in response. "Matias Romano. Our cousin. I know you've been away from the family scene for a while, but you remember Matias, don't you?"

Catarina ignored Filipe's remark. She carried enough guilt for keeping away from the family without needing reminders. "What room did you put him in?"

"I put him in the east wing, away from you. The guest bedroom facing the rear court."

"You gave him a room in the east wing?" For sure she'd run into the man even with him on the other side of the house.

13

Filipe looked up. "Should I have put him in the servants' quarters? Oh that's right, I don't have any." His mouth pressed in a straight line. "Don't be such a snob, Catarina. The attic is unfurnished, and the room off the kitchen is too small for someone staying this long."

Was she being a snob, or did she simply have a higher common sense?

"But you're leaving me with a stranger," she argued. How could he not see her point of view?

"The Silvas are here too."

"Not on the weekends."

Filipe gestured at the tablet sitting on the dresser. "Their phone number is on the list of important contacts. You can call them, and they'll be here in twenty minutes or less. Sete Fontes is not too far."

"It will still just be me and this guy in the house."

"I doubt you'll see him that much, with him so busy and you on the opposite side."

The farther from her, the better. "I'm not so sure about this new guy. I caught him watching me throw up by the rose bushes."

"You're still puking? I thought you were feeling better." Filipe opened the door, and they both exited the room.

She followed him to the landing. "So did I, but apparently not." She'd spent the last month and a half in close proximity to the bathrooms in the house. Today was the first day she'd ventured outside in a long time, and her moment of humiliation had been witnessed by a strange man. Just her luck.

Filipe stopped before descending. "Are you all right? You can't afford to lose any more weight. You should probably go to a doctor to see what's wrong with you."

Catarina sidled a hand over her still-flat belly and quickly moved it to her hip. "I'm pretty sure I'm on the mend." She could blame it on her little stowaway, even if she didn't tell Filipe. Kind of ironic that she'd finally lost the five kilos Juan-Carlos had nagged her about.

She flinched at the thought. Where had that come from? She didn't want to spare him any thoughts. He didn't deserve them.

Filipe watched her but didn't say anything. He probably regretted taking in a long-lost cousin who came with so much baggage. If Catarina had another choice, she'd take it, but she had nowhere else to go. She was much like the baby she carried: clandestine and totally dependent on someone else for the most basic needs.

They walked through the kitchen and stopped outside the back door.

Filipe playfully pulled a lock of her hair. "You take care of yourself, and don't get in too much trouble."

Catarina rolled her eyes. "You're just my cousin, not my older brother." The five-year gap between them had been more noticeable when they were children.

"I'm exactly the same age as Tiago. But maybe I'll call him instead." He smirked.

"Don't you dare." She leaned on the open jamb as he crossed the paved path to the rear courtyard toward the garage. "Are you taking the Audi or the Jeep?"

Filipe held up his keys. "The Jeep. Afonso has the keys to the Ford, and the Audi is there for you."

"Not funny," she called back to him.

Minutes later, the red jeep rolled out of the garage and Filipe waved at her. She held a hand up in return, unable to the hold back the small smile that pulled at the corners of her mouth when he honked the horn before disappearing around the house.

Catarina walked back to her bedroom. Two questions came to her mind. What was she going to do with herself without her cousin around?

And how was she going to avoid the man who'd just moved in?

CHAPTER TWO

$\mathcal{C}$atarina woke to her bedroom flooded in indirect light. This was the only suite in the house, with the bathroom, walk-in closet, and seating area to the right and the bedroom itself to the left, including a few windows facing west. The bed sat between the two walls. Through the large, naked panes, the sun's rays bounced on the pale gray walls and across the white coverlet.

She peeked at the digital clock on the bed side table and groaned at the late hour. Another morning spent in bed. This pregnancy sapped all her energy. She'd never been a morning person, but sleeping past eleven every morning was beyond her own standards. It didn't help that she'd gotten up twice during the night to go to the bathroom. Once she'd woken with the sounds of a distant piano, but she'd dismissed it as part of a weird dream and had fallen right back to sleep.

Her stomach grumbled, and she slipped a hand over it. At least, she'd remembered to place some Maria crackers in the bedside table drawer, as she'd read somewhere on the internet how it helped stave off nausea. Slowly, she opened the drawer and reached for the package. She took a bite from one and then stopped. How was she going to eat without leaving crumbs on the bed? Leaning over the edge of the bed, Catarina munched for a few minutes, hoping it would be enough. She'd deal with the crumbs on the floor later.

After a moment, she sat gingerly in bed, waiting for her stomach to rebel. When it didn't, she rose and approached the window overlooking the front yard. She unlatched the lock. Her eyes widened at the change: the sprouted grass was gone, now neatly mowed in a concentric pattern around the circle drive. On the wide lawn past the driveway, alternating rows of mowed grass marked the rectangular area bordering the old garden, which remained the same. But the hedgerows had been trimmed neatly, in wide contrast to the tangled mess of roses.

The new groundskeeper was keeping busy. Maybe Filipe was right and she wouldn't run into the guy after all.

As she got up to dress for the day, her stomach clenched, and she ran to the en suite bathroom. Fortunately, the vomiting didn't last long as she'd only had a couple of crackers. She brushed her teeth, then dressed in jeans and a loose top. For the time being, her wardrobe still fit.

Without the sounds of Filipe working on a project or playing music on his phone, the old house was quiet. The caretakers, Dona Madalena and Senhor Francisco, had left yesterday, as they usually did for the weekends. In the past few weeks since she'd arrived at Sunset Manor, Catarina had relied on Filipe to cook until Dona Madalena returned on Mondays. But now Catarina was on her own. The night before she'd fixed a frozen meal for dinner, but she'd barely picked at it. Having a personal chef on hand was one of the luxuries she missed. It was all in the past, and she'd do well to keep it there.

Catarina found clean dishes on the dish rack. The man had been in the kitchen to eat already. She'd heard him climb the stairs on his way to his bedroom in the evening yesterday but still hadn't seen him since their encounter in the old rose garden. Deep down, she was curious about him but not enough to seek him out. Nothing good would come of it.

Despite her lack of appetite, Catarina drew the carton of milk from the refrigerator and a roll from the freezer. After exactly ten seconds in the microwave, the roll was ready for a pat of butter. Maybe not the most nutritious breakfast, but with a weak stomach, she didn't dare eat anything heavier. She cut the prenatal vitamin in half and swallowed it carefully.

The vitamin container was fast approaching the one-third mark; she had maybe enough for two more weeks. Catarina sighed. She had to find a doctor in Castelo Branco soon. And after, she'd have to find a way to get there without raising suspicions.

The rest of the day passed too slowly. She'd been relying on Filipe more than she'd noticed, and his absence was harder than she'd predicted. Reading, napping, and watching comedies on Filipe's tablet only filled part of the time, and the customary walk was out of the question as she didn't want to risk running into Filipe's groundskeeper. After rifling through some drawers in the kitchen, she found a lined spiral notebook and a pencil. It would have to do for now. She hadn't sketched in a while, but her fingers itched for something to do.

By the time she lifted her head from the paper, the sun slanted through the windows and changed the color of the walls into an almost-peach hue. She'd skipped an afternoon snack in favor of a few crackers again, but she'd have to venture downstairs for dinner.

The lights were on in the kitchen, and the most delicious smell permeated the air. Catarina paused to inhale. The smell was robust, full, and with a hint of spice, and her stomach grumbled. On the granite counter in the center island, a table for one had been set at the far end: a full plate, a bottle of dark beer, flatware, and a paper napkin.

There was no one in sight.

When her stomach grumbled one more time, Catarina approached the island where a platter with cubed roasted potatoes and asparagus spears sat to one end. Despite the delicious smell, her weak stomach protested at the sight. How could she be hungry and queasy at the same time?

"You're welcome to join me for dinner."

Catarina yelped and jumped back.

A man stood by the glass sliding doors that led to the rear courtyard. The same man she'd seen yesterday.

The woman's face turned scarlet. Had she been about to eat the food? She was the one he'd seen by the old rose garden. He walked toward the sink, and she took a step back. Afonso dropped the tongs at the bottom of the sink to be washed later and took the plate with the grilled steaks to the counter. What was she doing in the house anyway?

"Who let you in? Does Filipe know you're here?"

She frowned and crossed her arms. "Of course Filipe knows I'm here."

Her attitude and tone were not what he'd expected. She was too sure of herself. He quirked an eyebrow at her.

She looked away for a moment.

"I have an extra steak. Would you like to join me?" He repeated the invitation and motioned toward the plate.

Her cheeks pinked up in her otherwise pale face. "Thank you."

Was that a yes or a no?

Just in case, he set another place at the counter as she watched him warily. Now that he had a better look, there was something about her that hinted she might still not be feeling well. As pretty as she was, her low weight and fatigued expression had him wondering about her health.

Afonso turned away from her. It wasn't his job to judge her. Or think about how pretty she was. And he still didn't know anything about her.

He sat down and motioned for her to serve herself. "I'm Afonso Cortez, by the way. I was hired yesterday."

"Yes, you're the new groundskeeper." She sat, then placed potatoes and two asparagus spears onto her plate.

Afonso slid the bottle of beer in her direction, and she shook her head. "I don't drink," she said quickly.

He cut into the steak. "Are you going to tell me what you're doing here?"

"I came to get something to eat."

Ironically, she'd barely touched her food. "I don't mean here in the kitchen. I mean here in the house." He took a swig from his beer, trying to be less conspicuous in the way he watched her. "So you know my name and what I'm doing here, but all I know about you is that you're related to the caretakers."

She glanced in his direction. "Dona Madalena and Senhor Francisco?" Her eyebrows knit together in a show of obvious confusion. "Why would I be related to them? I'm Filipe's cousin."

Afonso stopped chewing. "He didn't mention any cousins. He said there was an old relative—" He stopped. "Are you the widow?"

She straightened in her seat and crossed her arms. "That's kind of rude to ask point-blank, don't you think?"

"Are you Filipe's widowed relative staying in the west wing?"

"I'd rather you don't refer to me as the widow."

In his mind, Afonso went through the conversation he'd had with Filipe yesterday. Filipe had never said his relative was an old lady. Afonso had assumed she was old since Filipe had said she was widowed. "I'm sorry. What's your name?"

"Catarina." She glanced at him. "Catarina Romano."

Afonso shook his head and almost laughed out loud. After the problems aboard the *Princess Catarina*, he'd had enough of Catarinas to last him a lifetime. And now he was living with one in a remote house.

"Are you laughing at me?" Her tone was decidedly not friendly.

"No." He was but not for the reasons she thought.

"I just saw you laughing. What do you have against me?"

"Not you in particular." He hesitated before going on. She'd probably think he was weird. "Just your name."

23

"Excuse me?" The incredulity and indignation in her voice were more apparent now.

Afonso shrugged. "The last Catarina I met didn't bring much luck." It was an understatement, but he didn't have to go into details.

"So does this aversion extend to other names or just mine?"

Afonso finished his steak. He was anxious to change the topic. With some luck, maybe she'd move on if he steered the conversation. "So you're Filipe's cousin? Are you Matias' cousin too?" She must be with the Romano last name.

Her expression remained guarded, but there was a hint of curiosity. "You've met Matias?"

"I have." Afonso wondered how much she knew about him. Was she aware the new groundskeeper had come straight from prison?

Afonso busied himself cleaning up while he decided what to do. She didn't say much and looked to be lost in her own thoughts for a little while, head down on her phone screen. He glanced at her, trying to assess her. What kind of woman was she? Being a Romano didn't mean she was as understanding as her male cousins. She looked to be a little younger than him, but he'd never been good at guessing a woman's age. She was pretty, but there was something about her— an uncertainty and sadness in her expression. Maybe it was the grief over her husband's death at such a young age that caused her to lose her appetite. Mourning and depression had a toll on physical health.

24

And why did she look so familiar? He was certain he'd seen her before—not at the property, but somewhere else. "Have we met before?" When she scowled, he hurried on to explain. "I don't mean yesterday, or even here at the manor. Not recently."

"Is that your version of a pickup line?" Her voice let him know what she thought of it.

"What? No." This was not going well. He blew out a breath and turned to her. "I don't know how much Filipe told you about me, but I don't want to be accused of hiding my past."

She lifted her head toward him and frowned.

Afonso went on, not giving her a chance to say anything until he was done. "Due to some bad choices, I was in prison for the past few months. But I paid my debt, was released, and I'm not on probation. I'm here to work and do the job your cousin hired me to do. I'll stay out of your way, if you stay out of mine. It's a big house, and I'll be working outdoors most of the time, so I'm sure we can each keep to our own business. Nonetheless, Filipe said if you need anything to let me know." He walked over to the refrigerator and showed her the magnetic notepad and pen he'd found in a drawer earlier. "You can leave me a note on this pad, and I'll make sure to check on it. Since I get up early and you don't, it might be the best way to communicate."

She jumped to her feet. "Did you just call me lazy?" She stepped away from him, her arms straight at her side and her hands fisted.

This is what he'd feared. Afonso raised his hands. "No, I didn't call you lazy. I meant that you don't have to get up early, if you don't have a reason to. It's totally up to you." He grabbed the pad and pen from the refrigerator and set them down on the nearby counter. "You don't have to use these either. I'm sure you can find me if you need anything."

She didn't look any less angry. Maybe it was best not to say anything else tonight.

He walked past her. "Good night."

She stood in the same spot, arms crossed, watching him guardedly. Afonso made his way to his bedroom.

As long as she didn't complain to Filipe. Afonso couldn't lose this job.

CHAPTER THREE

$\mathcal{A}$fonso hadn't seen Catarina Romano in two days. She'd been effectively avoiding him, but he couldn't shake the feeling that something wasn't right.

After meeting Francisco and Madalena Silva on Monday, Afonso had been relieved for the caretakers' presence at the manor, a sort of buffer between him and Catarina. Senhor Francisco and he had been busy coordinating their schedules and working new to-do lists for the property. Dona Madalena's responsibilities kept her to the house, with the cleaning and the cooking, and he'd seen her talking with Catarina a few times.

But the Silvas had left on Thursday for a family event, and the house was too silent since then. Afonso couldn't find any evidence of Catarina being around, not even in the kitchen. Dona Madalena had left some meals to warm up, and it didn't look like anyone else was using them except him. Didn't Catarina come down to eat?

He ate quickly and cleaned up after himself, placing the leftovers in a glass container in the refrigerator. Afonso went through the house, checking to see if everything was in order. The work on the north lawn had kept him busy, but it was now done. He'd mowed one area at least the size of a football field, if not larger, trimmed all the edges, cleared the irrigation system, and fertilized the whole yard. He still needed to patch the bald spots, for which he needed new sod. A trip to Castelo Branco would take care of it. He had to make a list first to make sure he didn't forget anything else.

The ground floor was in order. He walked through the music room and spared a quick glance at the piano, not letting himself linger on it. It didn't seem like Catarina had come by the library. Afonso had been using it as a headquarters of sorts, referring back to the tablet with all the landscaping plans and to the maps Filipe had left for reference. Afonso had added notes and new files, including his cleaning and restoration schedule for each area, along with the shared schedule with the caretaker. Every morning before leaving the house, he checked off the work he'd done the day before and made himself a note for what needed to be done next.

He skipped the list for now. He'd come back to it before going to bed.

When he arrived at the first floor, he stopped to listen at the top of the stairs. He had yet to venture to the west wing; he hadn't needed to.

He didn't know which room was hers, but, from the layout of the house and what Filipe had said, she was probably in the master bedroom at the far end of the hallway.

The other bedrooms had doors ajar and were unoccupied and unfurnished, like most of the house. A large bathroom stood in between. In the east wing, where he was staying, a similar size bathroom serviced the two smaller bedrooms, one of which was his.

At the double door, he hesitated. She wouldn't welcome seeing him. But he had to make sure she was all right, and he'd risk her anger for his peace of mind.

Afonso rapped on the door and called her name, then waited.

Nothing.

Could she be outside and he'd miss seeing her?

"Catarina?" He knocked again.

After knocking again and calling her name with no response, Afonso tried the handle. The door was unlocked, and it turned easily. It was late in the day, and the remaining sun, low and still plenty warm, slanted through the windows and across the wood floor. The bedroom was sparsely furnished, and the gray walls took a peach tint at this time of day. A large bed sat against the south wall between two windows, piled high with white bedding and pillows strewn on its surface. A wardrobe, a stuffed chair by the west wall, and a wooden stool by the bed failed to fill the large space. On the other side, the door was ajar to the ensuite bathroom, saving him from knocking there too.

Afonso stood at the entrance a moment longer, taking in the lack of personal belongings and the stale air that filled the space. On impulse, he walked to the nearest window and pulled up on the sash, letting in the sweet evening breeze. When he turned around to leave, the mound of messed bedclothes moved, and a toe peeked out. He stopped.

She was there, one with the rolled sheets and the messed-up bedcovers, white fabric on pale skin. How could he have missed the shallow breathing and the woman sleeping uneasily a few paces away from him?

Afonso stood by the bed. Was she asleep or sick? "Catarina."

She didn't respond.

He called her name again, louder, leaning closer to the bed.

She moaned and turned to his side.

"Catarina, have you been sick?"

She mumbled.

Afonso knelt by the bed and kept his hands away from her. "I'm sorry I came to your bedroom. I just want to make sure you're okay."

"Is Juan-Carlos here yet?" Her voice rasped, and she coughed.

Afonso dragged a stack of pillows against the headboard and helped her up. When she raised herself on her elbows, she went down again.

There was definitely something going on. Her skin felt papery and warm to the touch, and her lips were dry. "When was the last time you had something to eat or drink?" He looked around for a glass, but there wasn't one there.

Afonso got up and found a glass in the bathroom with a toothbrush in it. He gave it a quick rinse and filled it halfway. It would have to do until he could get something better in her.

He brought the glass to her lips. "Little sips."

She choked, and he drew the glass away as she slid back into the bed.

Guilt pricked at him. She must have had a relapse. Filipe had mentioned she'd been sick, but Afonso had forgotten to check on her after the Silvas left. He took her pulse and counted the beats. He didn't know her well enough to assess her mental state, but the physical signs pointed at severe dehydration. Did he have the means to help her regain her health? Should he call Filipe?

He didn't know how long she'd been like this. A couple of days or more? It would be better to err on the side of caution and get her to medical help. Maybe it was a case of severe dehydration or maybe it was something more. He wasn't a doctor and he couldn't diagnose her. He'd take her to the emergency room and call Filipe from there once she was admitted.

Afonso assisted her in drinking a few more sips of water, but even that seemed to tax her energy.

"Just rest here, Catarina. I'm going to get the car around closer to the door, and I'll get you to see the doctor."

She made a sound, but Afonso couldn't tell if she'd understood, or even heard him.

"Filipe," she called, her voice just above a whisper.

He stopped at the door and turned to her. "Yes?" It would take too long to correct her.

"Don't tell Juan-Carlos I'm not feeling well," she whispered in the same scratchy voice.

Who was Juan-Carlos? Filipe hadn't mentioned anyone by that name. Could it be her decesead husband? Was she confused or hallucinating? "I won't," he assured her.

Once in the garage, he decided to get the truck instead and drove it to the front of the house, where it was closer to bring her from the bedroom.

In her bedroom, Afonso wrapped her in the flat sheet, not knowing what she wore underneath the pile of bedclothes. He carried her to the back seat, more slowly than he would have liked, but taking care not to jostle her too much.

The normal one-hour drive to Castelo Branco took him only forty minutes. When he arrived at the regional hospital, he was relieved the emergency personnel took Catarina in right away.

"What's her name?" the on-call nurse asked.

"Catarina Romano." She'd never mentioned her married name, but nowadays some women didn't change their surname when they married.

32

When he hesitated going past the admitting door, the nurse turned back to him. "You can come in with her. Just stay out of the way."

Afonso rubbed his neck. "I'm not—I'm not family."

"Are you her fiancé?"

He shook his head.

"Boyfriend?"

"No, nothing like that. I work at the house where she's staying. Her cousin owns it, and he hired me. Is it serious? Do I need to call him?"

"I'll let you know after the doctor is done assessing her."

For the first thirty minutes, Afonso sat on a plastic chair in the waiting room. In the far corner, away from the few others that had been brought there tonight, he rested his elbows on his knees and leaned forward, counting the ceramic tiles on the floor. When he asked for an update, the nurses told him to wait.

An hour later, Afonso had nodded off against the wall when someone touched him on the shoulder. He jumped forward in the chair.

"Follow me," the nurse said.

She took him past the swinging door. "Wait here."

The nurses' station stood to the left of the wide hallway. A row of sick bays, most with the curtains drawn open, lined up to the right side.

After a few minutes, a doctor approached him. "What's your relationship to the patient?" He consulted the clipboard in his hand.

"None. I work at the house where she's staying. Do you think I need to call her family?"

"I can't discuss her case with you then. All I can tell you is that we're keeping her overnight."

The doctor walked away, leaving Afonso with his questions unanswered.

A petite nurse approached him. "If you're brief, you can come say hi to her before we take her upstairs."

Did he want to talk to Catarina? Maybe he could ask her if she wanted him to call Filipe.

He slipped past the curtain. At first she looked to be sleeping, but she turned her head toward him. An IV needle was hooked to her arm, and she had an oxygen hose in her nose. Other nearby equipment monitored her state.

"Was it you who brought me here?" Her voice was low but firmer than before, more coherent.

Afonso nodded. "Do you remember anything at all?"

"Not really. Did you call Filipe?"

"Not yet, but I will."

She held a hand up a bit before letting it drop to the bed. "Don't call him."

Afonso raised an eyebrow.

"By the time he gets here, I'll be home and feeling better." She paused to take a breath. "Don't call him, please."

"Anyone else you want me to call?" Did she have no family she wanted to come?

She shook her head.

The nurse entered then. "Okay, time's up."

Afonso didn't know what to say to Catarina. "Hope you'll feel better soon." She hadn't said what was wrong with her, and he didn't have the right to ask.

"Wait."

He turned back.

She looked toward the nurse, and the nurse busied herself at the opposite corner, giving them a false sense of privacy.

Afonso stepped closer to the bed.

"Can you—do you think you could give me a ride home when I'm released?" Her tone was insecure, almost as if she didn't dare ask him.

"I was planning on it." Did she think he was going to leave her at the hospital with no means to get back?

"Can I call you when I'm ready to go?"

"Sure. I'll leave my number with the nurses."

"I'd like to have it." She lowered her eyes. "If you don't mind."

Afonso looked around for a pen and a piece of paper, hiding his surprise at her request. The young nurse handed him her pen and a small pad. He wrote his name and number and handed the square to Catarina.

She held on to it. "Thank you."

"No problem. Call me when you're ready. I'll need an hour to get here," he added.

He stopped at the nurses' station and left his number, with instructions to call if something happened. They should have someone's number even if he wasn't related to Catarina. Maybe she didn't want her family to come, but he wouldn't leave her stranded.

The vulnerability in her expression had touched him. She was not the same person he'd met around the manor in the past two weeks. Whatever sickness she had, it had humbled her.

But there was something more in her eyes. Something that troubled him.

Catarina smoothed the piece of paper between her palm and the thin cotton blanket. It was more than a piece of a paper with a name and a phone number written on it. It was a connection; the only one she had right now.

Afonso was kinder than she'd expected. Kinder than she deserved, after the way she'd treated him.

"We'll be transferring you upstairs within the hour," the nurse said after taking Catarina's blood pressure again. "Can I get you anything?"

"No, thank you."

After the nurse left, Catarina wiped the single tear that had leaked without permission.

She was exhausted. In body, in mind, and even in heart. A deep weariness had taken over her being.

The last few days were a blur, and she didn't have a clear memory of Afonso bringing her to the hospital. He'd said he'd need an hour to drive back, so she must be in Castelo Branco.

He'd driven her to the hospital in Castelo Branco, and he was coming back to take her home. Not her home, but the only one she had at the moment.

She had misjudged Afonso Cortez.

Unbidden and unwanted, the memory came to her of the time she'd had an emergency appendectomy four years ago. Juan-Carlos hadn't been home, and the chauffeur had taken her to the hospital. She'd expected Juan-Carlos to come see her when he found out about her surgery, but he didn't come. When she called him to say she was being released, he sent the chauffeur to pick her up. Then he'd left an hour after she arrived home, saying she needed to rest and he was just in the way. She had cried all night, more from the disappointment than the post-op pain.

Today, a stranger had treated her with more compassion and kindness than her own husband ever had.

They moved her to a small two-bed room and placed her by the window. Relieved to see the other bed empty, Catarina tried to relax and settle in for the night.

Between the nurses coming to take her vitals every hour and her guilty conscience keeping her awake, sleep eluded her.

In the early morning she was feeling marginally better. Not yet to full strength, but whatever they'd put in the IV had made a difference already. She even ate some of the light breakfast they brought her, and by the time the doctor came to see her after ten o'clock, she told him she was ready to go home.

"Not so fast. I'd like to keep you for a few more hours and make sure you won't have a relapse." He pulled up a chair. "Let's talk about what happened. How did you get to this point of dehydration?"

Catarina turned her face to the other side for a moment. The doctor looked to be in his midfifties, about the same age as her dad. She was twenty-five years old; definitely not a child. So why did she feel like she was being scolded for not taking care of herself?

"I've been throwing up quite a bit, and then I lost my appetite. And I'm always tired." So tired.

He opened the folder in his hand. "We ran some blood tests. Your hCG levels indicate you might be further along in your pregnancy, but your small size is confusing. Obstetrics is not my specialty." He looked up at her. "You do know you're pregnant, right?"

She nodded. Sometimes she didn't want to remember she was pregnant, but it was hard to forget when her own body betrayed her.

"I'm going to prescribe anti-nausea medicine for when it gets really bad. I'll give you some samples to take home until you can get to a pharmacy." He scribbled something. "Take them with food. And a prescription for prenatal vitamins. Take them at night, with dinner. You'll be more likely to keep them down. Carry a water bottle with you. Stay away from sodas, coffee, and caffeinated drinks. Fruit juices in moderation. Plenty of rest and eating at regular times will help too. Do you have an obstetrician?"

"Not yet."

He turned a page in the folder and scanned it for information. "Where do you live?"

"In Sete Fontes." It was the closest village to Filipe's house.

"You'll have to come to Castelo Branco. You won't find any doctors closer. I can give you a couple of recommendations if you'd like."

"Yes, please."

He made another annotation. "They'll give it to you when you're released." He paused. "Make an appointment as soon as possible. If I don't see you before you leave, good luck, Catarina. Take care of yourself and your baby."

"Thank you, doctor."

After he left, the day nurse came in to replace the IV bag and check her vital signs. Again.

"Lunch will be here soon, and the doctor ordered you to eat all of it."

"I'll try."

The nurse adjusted the flow from the IV bag to the tube. "If you don't eat, you'll have to stay another night."

The stern look on her face didn't leave any doubts about how serious she was. Catarina rushed to amend herself. "Okay, I'll eat everything."

After lunch, she napped. She'd eaten all the food on the tray, and even though there hadn't been much of it, it had taken a long time to go through it.

When the nurse came to change the IV bag once more, she promised it would be the last one.

"I need to call my ride to let him know I'll be going home soon." Catarina hoped Afonso would answer the phone.

The nurse pushed the old-fashioned phone closer to Catarina. "I forgot to tell you. A man called when you were sleeping."

Catarina stilled. "A man?"

"Afonso Cortez? Do you know him?"

"Yes, he's the one giving me the ride. What did he say?"

"He just asked about you and how you were doing." She picked up the half-filled water pitcher. "I'll bring you some fresh water."

Catarina turned the words in her mind. Afonso Cortez had called asking about her. Try as she might, she couldn't understand why he cared. He was a contradiction: a man who'd been in prison for committing a crime, and a man who rushed her to the hospital and called to find out how she was doing.

Maybe Filipe was right and she'd judged Afonso too harshly.

After another short nap, she called Afonso and asked him to bring some of her loungewear clothes to change into. When he showed up, at the exact time he'd said he'd be there, he carried a shopping bag.

40

He set it down at the foot of the bed. "I'm sorry, but I didn't feel right about going through your wardrobe. I hope this will do." He looked down, then away to the window before looking back at her. "I'll wait for you in the hallway." He turned and left quickly.

Was that a blush creeping up his neck? She didn't know him, but it looked like Afonso Cortez was blushing.

She opened the bag and pulled out a small bundle wrapped in white tissue paper. When she drew the layers back, silky pink fabric sat inside. Catarina picked it up and held a beautiful satin kimono-style robe in front of her. It had a row of magnolias all around the hem and on the cuffs of the long sleeves and enough length to reach past mid-calf. It was appropriate for her to wear on the way home and it would serve well as a cover-up. But it was something so unexpected.

So thoughtful of Afonso, who hadn't wanted to riffle through her drawers in the wardrobe.

The nurse came to unhook the IV from her and disconnect the rest of the equipment. "The doctor already signed your discharge papers." She read the instructions to Catarina and had her sign at the bottom. "An orderly will come with the wheelchair shortly."

"Do I really need to leave in a wheelchair?"

The nurse gave her a stern look. "That is not open for discussion."

She helped Catarina to the edge of the bed and put the plastic bag with her possessions—the mis-

41

matched pajamas she'd arrived in—within her reach. The nurse pulled the curtain around Catarina's bed and left.

Catarina sat there and gave herself a few minutes to adjust. It had been a hard week, and there was a lot for her to take in, a lot to think about. Especially about Afonso. She changed from the hospital gown into her pajamas, being careful not to stand too long and risk a fall.

Then she reached for the kimono and slipped it on. It slid smoothly against her skin. She pulled at the lapels and cinched it tightly to hide what she wore underneath. She sorely needed a shower, and there was nothing she could do about her limp hair, but wearing the kimono made her feel less self-conscious of the state she was in.

When the orderly wheeled her to the front of the hospital, Afonso stood by the truck, the passenger door wide open. Afonso gently took the plastic bag from her and placed it in the back seat. Then he reached for her elbow and helped her to the front.

He walked around and buckled himself behind the wheel. After looking ahead for a moment, he turned to her. "Let me know if we need to stop along the way."

Catarina held his gaze. "I think I'll be okay."

He nodded and turned the ignition on.

The ride home was quiet and long. Somehow she fell asleep, and Afonso nudged her awake when they arrived. Catarina managed to climb the stairs to the first floor and take a quick shower, using the built-in seat to steady herself. She changed into clean pajamas and dried her hair. The pink satin kimono was draped at the foot of the bed where she'd left it, and she slipped it back on.

Catarina stilled when she approached her bed. It had been made, the sheets changed. Dona Madalena and Senhor Francisco wouldn't be back until Wednesday, as they'd repeatedly told Afonso and Catarina before they left.

Afonso had done it. He'd changed the sheets, washed them, and made the bed.

She swallowed past the lump in her throat. When would this man stop surprising her?

A knock sounded at the door.

"Come in."

Afonso entered the bedroom carrying a tray. "Do you have your medication with you?" He set the tray on the nearby chair.

"They're in the bag. I'll get them." She didn't want him to see the sample box of prenatal vitamins.

On the tray, a small pitcher of water, a glass, and a cloth napkin crowded one side. A soup plate with vegetable soup and a piece of toast took the rest of the space.

Catarina looked up at Afonso and hitched an eyebrow, but he seemed to anticipate her question.

"You shouldn't take your pills on an empty stomach." He gestured at the plate. "It's just a simple vegetable soup. Fresh. I made it this morning."

"You made soup from scratch?"

He shrugged. "I called the nurse to see what you could eat, and she suggested simple meals to build your strength." He took a step back and slipped his hands in his pockets, then drew them out. "I'll come back later for the tray."

Catarina looked between him and the tray once more. "Why are you doing this for me?"

He frowned at her. "Why wouldn't I?"

She could think of a few reasons.

Just as he reached the door, she called after him. "Thank you."

Afonso's expression softened. "You're welcome."

"Thank you for everything," Catarina added.

A simple thanks wasn't enough.

CHAPTER FOUR

*C*atarina woke up the next morning to the droning sound of the lawn mower on the south side of the house.

Since Afonso's arrival, the grounds had never looked so well. He'd cleared the deadwood and weeds in the rose garden but still hadn't pruned the rose bushes. There was so much to do just around the house, she couldn't even imagine all the work the property required. Filipe had tried to take her on a tour when she first arrived but she hadn't been interested, what with Juan-Carlos' funeral still so fresh in her mind. The financial mess that resulted from his death had been just as hard to deal with.

From the window, she could see Afonso on a riding lawn mower, finishing up the last row. He pulled on a lever to stop the blades and drove the mower to the gravel path, then turned it off. Once off the seat, he walked in front of the area as if checking the preciseness of each row he'd just mowed. He was meticulous and took his job seriously. Catarina couldn't help noticing the way his blue tank top showed off his well-defined upper arms and shoulders. What was his job before being in prison? Or had he worked out while serving his sentence?

She pushed the thought away. It was none of her business how Afonso had occupied his time inside, or how good he looked in that shirt.

When he turned to hop back on the mower, he saw Catarina at the window and waved at her. She raised her hand.

A few minutes later, a soft knock sounded at the door.

"Just a minute," she replied as she hastily pulled on the pink kimono before opening the door.

Afonso stood barefoot in the hallway, and her eyes went to his feet, trying to distract herself from how much better that stupid blue shirt looked on him from up close.

"I didn't want to track dirt and grass clippings through the house." His eyes strayed to her collarbone, and he quickly brought them back up. "I saw you're up. What would you like for breakfast?"

Catarina's jaw slacked for a moment before she caught herself. "Are you offering to make breakfast for me?"

"Just until you're feeling better."

"You didn't have to interrupt your work and come inside to make me breakfast. I'll be okay."

"Well, I'm already here, and I had to refill my water bottle anyway. What would you like?"

"I—I really hadn't thought about it yet." She'd been too busy ogling him from the window.

"Scrambled eggs? Oatmeal? Are you hungry?"

"No, I'm not very hungry. I mean, I know I have to eat, but maybe I'll grab a piece of toast after I take a shower."

"You need something with more nutrition than a slice of bread. I'll bring you a tray."

Before she had the chance to protest, Afonso was halfway down the staircase.

Catarina closed the door. Had she just discussed breakfast with Afonso Cortez at her bedroom door?

After her shower, she found a pair of black yoga pants at the bottom of the wardrobe and a striped button shirt that could use a touch of ironing. She actually needed to spend some time in the laundry room today. No laundry maids in this house.

She rolled up the sleeves and untucked the shirt. Her hands smoothed down the front and stopped on her belly. For the time being, it was still flat, but soon she'd start showing and she'd need to buy maternity clothes.

Maybe if she hurried she could still catch Afonso before he brought the tray up from the kitchen.

When she opened the door, the breakfast tray sat on a wooden chair in the middle of the hallway in front of her room.

47

It was a simple breakfast, but he'd definitely put some thought into it—a scrambled egg with a side of fresh cheese, a small bowl of oatmeal with a sliced banana, sprinkled with brown sugar and cinnamon. For drinking, a tall glass of orange juice and a glass of milk.

Catarina carried the tray inside and set it on the bed, then dragged the chair in. She transferred the tray to the chair and sat at the edge of the bed.

There was a note on the tray, and she read it while eating the egg.

Hope you like eggs and oatmeal. If not, let me know what you prefer next time.

Next time, she'd make her own breakfast.

This is my cell number. Text me when you're ready for lunch.

His number followed. She still had the paper with his number that he'd given her at the hospital. Maybe he thought she didn't have it anymore.

The eggs were perfect, especially with the fresh cheese. She'd never tried the combination before, but she liked it. She usually preferred blueberries on oatmeal—a habit learned from Juan-Carlos—but the brown sugar with cinnamon and banana went really well. In the end, she ate more than she thought she would.

Had Afonso worked as a chef? How did he know to cook so well?

Thankfully, she'd remembered to take the anti-nausea pill and was able to keep down the breakfast.

Afterward, she picked up her phone and typed a text to Afonso.

Thanks for breakfast.

He replied almost immediately. **You're welcome. Hope it was okay.**

It was great. But I don't expect you to cook for me. That's not what Filipe hired you for. You won't need to come in to make lunch.

I'll be coming in to make lunch for myself. You're welcome to join me. See you then.

Catarina stared at the screen. Was he always like this?

She took the tray to the kitchen and washed the dishes. That was the least she could do.

The laundry room stood on the other side of the kitchen, opposite the butler's pantry. She found everything she'd need to wash, dry, and iron—even a dryer and a steaming machine—and returned to the bedroom for her dirty clothes. On the floor, the lined notebook and pencil peeked from under the bed, and she placed them on top of the basket.

For all the updates Filipe had done to the house, a laundry room on the ground floor was not enough. Not wanting to climb the staircase again while the first load washed, Catarina walked around the ground floor until she found a sofa in the old library and plopped down on it. Why hadn't Filipe furnished the house yet? The library was almost as far from the laundry room as it was from her bedroom, but at least she didn't have to negotiate the grand staircase.

The pencil was hard and the paper too cheap, but she drew a perspective of the library with the bookcase full of old books, the fireplace lit, and a shaggy dog sleeping in front of it. She cocked her head. The angles were off. When was the last time she'd sketched? She couldn't even remember.

When she stood to place the second load in the dryer, the door to the courtyard opened and closed and a set of quick steps sounded across the tiled floor. Catarina walked to the kitchen, where she found Afonso at the sink.

He wiped his hands on a kitchen towel and frowned at her. "You're down here."

Catarina pulled out a chair at the table and sat down. "I had to do some laundry."

"Are you feeling strong enough for that?"

"As long as I'm careful going up and down the stairs."

He pulled out a pot from the lower cupboard. "I'll have lunch ready soon. I'll call you when it's ready."

"I'll stay, if you don't mind. I still have a load in the dryer."

He popped into the pantry for a moment and came out with a large onion in his hand. "I was surprised to find a dryer in the laundry room, but I must admit it's very convenient."

While the whole country still dried clothes on the line, she couldn't remember the last time she'd done that. Juan-Carlos had dryers in all the houses and apartments, even though he left the laundry to be done by the maids.

For the next few minutes, Afonso entered and exited the pantry as he gathered ingredients for whatever he had planned to make for lunch.

She had so many questions. The man intrigued her, more than anyone had in a long time. As she watched him capably navigating the kitchen, she couldn't help but wonder who he really was, what he did.

Afonso gave the pan a stir and glanced at Catarina. "If you want to know anything about me, just ask, Catarina. I've got nothing to hide. I don't lie, and I don't keep secrets."

Was it so obvious that she had questions, or was he a mind reader?

He reached out a hand to the spice rack and unscrewed the cap from a small bottle. Then he brought it to his nose and took a whiff. An eyebrow went up, and his expression brightened with satisfaction as he poured some of the spice in his palm and added it to the dish.

She watched him quietly for a moment. Lies came easy to her, and secrets were a way of life. "Do you hold every one by the same standards?"

"Not anymore. I learned my lesson the hard way."

He held her gaze, and Catarina found herself unable to look away. The expression in his brown eyes was assured and unmistakable. When was the last time she'd seen such openess in a man? Her dad and brothers, for sure, and the rest of the Romano men. But it had been a while since she'd been around them, or any of the family. The regret gnawed at her. She had so much to make up for. Deceit had been a normal way of life for so long that she barely remembered what honesty looked like in a man.

Did he truly not mind her curiosity?

Afonso regarded Catarina seated to his right at the corner of the bar.

She had questions.

He'd served a simple meal of boiled potatoes and broiled fish on a bed of sautéed onions, accompanied with a salad, something that had been quick to prepare but still provided good nutrition. She'd barely eaten anything, claiming she was still full from the large breakfast. He didn't know what she looked like in full health, but her face was still pale, making him wonder how recovered she was from whatever had made her so sick over the weekend.

What was Catarina's story? Why was she staying at Sunset Manor? The questions kept coming back to him.

As curious as he was about her, Afonso wouldn't let it show. Her eyes were too guarded, as if she feared someone getting too close and finding too much.

After discussing the merits of broiled fish over fried, he set the fork down. "I'm sure my broiling techniques are fascinating, but I can tell you have questions that are not related to how I cook fish."

His comment brought a pale smile to her lips. She took a bite and then rested the utensils on the edge of the plate. Even with his permission, she still hesitated.

"I meant what I said. You can ask me anything," he repeated.

At last, she raised her eyes to him. "What happened?"

Afonso pushed his plate away and sat back. "You mean, what happened to land me in jail?"

A light blush tinted her cheeks, and she nodded, tucking away her hair behind her ear.

"I was too naïve." An understatement. "I chose to believe the words of a woman who hadn't given me any reason to." He let out a long breath. "I guess I fancied myself in love with her and developed some warped sense of loyalty. When I found out what she intended to do, I kept quiet and didn't warn anyone of her plans, didn't do anything to stop her. Her actions caused damage and put the lives of one hundred and seventy people in danger." To this day, the gross lapse of judgment he suffered during that last cruise aboard the *Princess Catarina* still made him angry. He'd fallen so fast for Anabela Rialto's words. "She ditched me at the first chance, and luckily I came to my senses and turned myself in within two days."

"And you were tried?"

"Tried and sentenced to nine months, but I got out

in five for good behavior." The longest five months of his life.

"And what happened to this woman?"

"Still at large. They haven't been able to find her." She deserved to be put away for what she'd done, but it wasn't up to him anymore. He was done with Anabela in his life.

"If I hadn't kept the secrets I knew, I could have prevented the whole thing." Lies never brought anything good. "When I got out, Captain Romano gave me this chance, and I took it."

Catarina straightened in her seat. "Captain Romano? One of my cousins?"

"Yes, Matias Romano. I worked with him aboard the *Princess Catarina*."

"Oh." Her expression sobered. "That's how you know Matias."

Afonso shrugged. "I wasn't very lucky with that Catarina, but it was partly my fault."

"Catarina wasn't a woman. It was a boat."

"A river cruise ship that your cousin captains."

"And he told you Filipe was hiring a groundskeeper to tend a property in the middle of nowhere."

He nodded. "Exactly what I needed."

"A place to start over," she said.

"Is that what Sunset Manor means to you too?"

Catarina's expression turned guarded immediately.

"I'm sorry. I shouldn't have asked." Just because he'd wanted to tell her about his past, didn't mean she wanted to tell him about hers.

She stood from the bar and took her plate to the sink. "I better finish my laundry. Thank you for lunch."

She'd picked around her plate, but hopefully the little she'd eaten was enough.

"You're welcome. I'll be at the north end of the property this afternoon, but I have my phone with me if you need anything."

"I'll be okay." She stopped at the door to the laundry room. "How big is it?"

He frowned. "How big is what?"

"The property. Filipe tried to take me on a tour when I arrived, but I wasn't much in the mood for it back then."

Having just buried her husband, he could understand why.

"The immediate grounds around the house comprise five hectares, with another ten suitable for farming or ranching."

Her eyes rounded. "I had no idea it was this large."

"I can take you on a tour if you want."

She stared back at him, and Afonso regretted the invitation. Of course she didn't want to go with him. "Or you can wait for Filipe next time he comes."

"He's too busy with his new project. I'd like to go but—do we have to walk?"

"There's an all-terrain vehicle, a four-wheel drive. It seats two people."

"I'd love to go then," she said at last.

Afonso nodded. "After dinner, when the weather is cooler." It had been unseasonably warm for late spring.

"Okay." She stared at him for a moment longer, then turned and left the room.

Afonso gathered the few dishes in the sink, filled it with water, and added a squirt of detergent.

Had he really offered to take Catarina on a tour of the property? She'd surprised him by saying yes.

What if it turned out to be a bad idea?

Maybe he shouldn't be looking forward to it so much.

CHAPTER FIVE

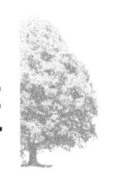

After washing, drying, and folding two loads of laundry—she'd left ironing for another day, if she got to it at all—Catarina had gone to her bedroom to lie down and rest.

But sleep hadn't come.

Her mind kept going to lunch with Afonso.

He hadn't minded her questions about his past, and almost seemed to welcome them.

He'd worked on a ship with her cousin Matias. No wonder Matias had recommended Afonso to Filipe.

What had Afonso done aboard? That hadn't come up. Maybe she'd ask him some other time.

She couldn't believe she'd asked Afonso for a tour of the grounds.

It must be loneliness and boredom. There was no one else around the house to talk to, and today she'd enjoyed the time she'd spent with Afonso.

There, she'd admitted it to herself.

Afonso Cortez was good company and an excellent cook.

She lay in bed for over two hours, then sat against the headboard and turned on the cell phone. What with being sick and the hospital stay, she'd forgotten to check the daily alerts. Before she gave in to the old habit, Catarina pressed the button and deleted the alert.

Nobody would come looking for Dulce Vega in this part of the country. The gossip rags believed her to be in southern Spain, and that was fine by her.

Juan-Carlos had nicknamed her Dulce when they met, the word for *sweet* in Spanish, and the name had stuck in his circle of friends and acquaintances. By the time they married, it was the only name the media knew her by, and Catarina hadn't minded the change. After all, she'd started a new life as the wife of a jet-setter, and a new name went along with it. So naïve. Though she kept the name, she soon learned she wasn't the only one he called sweet.

Castelo Branco was far away from all that, and Sunset Manor was even farther. Besides, she didn't look like the same woman who'd been married to Juan-Carlos de Aragón y Vega. She'd lost some weight due to the morning sickness, her hair had returned to its natural brown without the regular blonde highlights, and her hands looked plain, void of fake red nails and gold rings. The only jewelry she had left was a pair of diamond stud earrings and her wedding band— pieces she'd been wearing when she'd left Lisbon in a hurry carrying only a suitcase.

She was so far from the woman she'd been before Juan-Carlos' death, she hardly recognized herself.

And she was beginning to like it.

Instead of waiting for Afonso to cook dinner, she could get one of the frozen dinners Dona Madalena had prepared and put it in the oven. Catarina supposed it was easy enough that even she couldn't mess it up.

She rummaged in the deep freezer until she found a dish she thought Afonso would like. She'd noticed he cooked healthy, balanced food. The instructions on the front were straightforward: turn the oven on to 160°C, leave it in for forty five minutes, cool for ten minutes before serving. It looked to be some potato and codfish dish; it should be okay for him.

While she waited for the oven to warm up, Catarina stepped outside into the rear courtyard. She walked to the railing overlooking the lawn. She hadn't seen this area for a while, but it looked like Afonso had mowed it recently too. To the other side of the path that led to the garage, a forgotten garden patch had a corner of revolved dirt where someone had started to pull the weeds.

How much work did Afonso have on his to-do list every day? No wonder Filipe had hired him to work for five months. There was so much to do.

She returned to the kitchen to find the oven ready. The tray went in, and she set the timer. As Catarina turned from the wall oven, she found Afonso entering the room wearing nothing but a bath towel low on his hips.

She stilled, and her mouth dropped open.

Afonso froze. "I thought you were napping." His dark hair was wet from the shower, and water droplets covered his shoulders, torso, and arms.

"I thought you were still outside." Her eyes strayed to his body, and she reluctantly brought them back up to his face.

Was that amusement in his expression? There was no mistake: she was caught openly admiring him. Could he tell the flush in her cheeks? Her internal temperature had suddenly risen, and she wished for a fan. Darn pregnancy hormones, inflating reactions out of proportion.

"I fell in a bog," Afonso said.

His voice brought Catarina back. "You fell in what?"

"A muddy pit. It was deeper than I thought, and it got me all dirty." He gestured to the next room. "I was on my way to the laundry room."

"The laundry room?" Why was she repeating everything he said? Where were the words that didn't make her sound stupid? She'd read about pregnancy brain, but this was ridiculous.

His hand went to the tucked-in towel on his hip.

She held her breath.

"To get my clothes. I'm going to the laundry room to get my clothes." He passed a hand through his hair and walked away. "I'll be right back."

"That's good. I'll just—I'll stay here."

Once Afonso cleared the doorway, Catarina ran her hands under cold water and pressed them to her cheeks.

What an idiot. As if she'd never seen a seminaked man. In her defense, it had been a while—between Juan-Carlos' absence and his preoccupation with impressing other women—and Afonso was in good shape. He didn't look bulked up like some guys did who went to the gym every day. Juan-Carlos even had a personal trainer for a while. But Afonso was taller and leaner than Juan-Carlos. So different from Juan-Carlos.

Stop. She had to stop comparing her late husband with her cousin's hired hand. No matter how nice Afonso was and how respected he made her feel. She had to.

"You okay?" Afonso's voice sounded behind her, and Catarina jumped. He was dressed in jeans and a dark blue T-shirt that fit him all too well. How had she not noticed before how attractive he was?

"Yes, I'm fine. Just checking the alarm on the oven to see if it's ready."

He raised an eyebrow. "All the way back from the sink?"

She fanned herself with her hand. "It's cooler over here." Could her reply have sounded any more ridiculous? She looked away to hide her embarrassment.

A smile tugged at the corner of his mouth. "Yeah, it is kind of hot in here."

61

If only the kitchen was the only hot thing.

How was she going to get through the rest of the evening without making a bigger fool of herself?

After the awkwardness of being caught in a towel, Afonso enjoyed dinner with Catarina. She was more relaxed tonight, despite not sharing any personal details from her past. He wouldn't force her to satisfy his curiosity. All in due time.

Afonso brought the four-wheeler from the barn and parked it in front of the back porch. She was waiting for him on the first step, hair pulled back into a ponytail.

It was just a ride around the property. Nothing more. He'd do well to remember that.

He hopped off and came around the ATV. "You ready?"

Catarina approached him. "It's bigger than I thought."

"It's safe. We won't be doing any off-roading. I'll stick to the paths, and we won't be gone too long, if it makes you uncomfortable."

"No, it's fine," she replied quickly. "I'd like to see the property so I can tell Filipe I've finally done it." She turned her attention to the vehicle. "Are there any rules on how to ride it?"

"Just center yourself on the seat and don't lean to the sides. I'll do the rest." He wasn't an expert, but he'd been riding it on the grounds since the first week he'd arrived. He climbed on and showed her where to place her foot so she could swing the other leg over the seat.

She watched him. "Where do I hold on?"

"You can grip the seat, like this." He scooted back and placed his fingers under the edge of the seat, then slid to the front again.

She still didn't get on. "But I could still fall backward if I lose my balance." She inspected the seat on the ATV once more.

"Yes, some people have a hard time keeping their balance while riding, so they just hold on to the driver."

Her eyes lifted to his. "You mean I hold on to you?"

The corner of his mouth rose. "I won't bite. I promise."

Her cheeks flushed. She glanced from him to the ATV once more, hesitation written all over her expression.

"Do you want to leave it for another day?" He wouldn't pressure her.

"No. Let's go." With resolve, she placed a hand on his shoulder and hopped on behind him. Her right hand came loosely around his hip and, when he peeked back at her, she gripped the seat with the other.

Afonso shifted the four-wheeler into gear, keeping his hand on the brake lever, then glanced over his shoulder. "Ready?"

Catarina nodded, and he released the brake and eased slowly into first gear to give her time to get used to the machine.

As they left the flatness of the rear lawn and started the gradual ascent toward the back of the property, he felt her slipping back in her seat, and he covered her hand with his over his middle for a brief moment. Catarina's other arm snaked around him with a firmer grip.

When the path opened up into two, Afonso turned over his shoulder so she could hear him over the rattling of the ATV. "I'm taking you to the back of the property first, where it borders with the forest. We'll loop around to the main gate and then end up at the house."

"Sounds good." Her breath brushed his ear, and the small hairs on his neck raised immediately. Afonso expelled a quick breath and concentrated on the ride instead of Catarina's soft body against his back.

It had been a while since he'd been this close to a woman. It wasn't an embrace, but it felt like one. Her earlier hesitancy was gone, replaced with a kind of trust that he knew what he was doing.

He had no clue. Other than driving the ATV and showing her cousin's property, Afonso didn't know what he was doing sitting close to this woman who was hiding from something she didn't want to talk about. That much he'd guessed.

Catarina touched his shoulder, and he slowed down.

She gestured toward the fence ahead. "The fence is down over there."

"Hold on," he said to her. He sped up a bit until they reached the spot she'd indicated.

He turned off the engine and got off. Catarina followed him.

On closer look, the fence wasn't down, but the wires had been cut clean through. This was a job done with wire cutters, not wires snapped by a large animal or some other natural force.

"Everything okay?" she asked.

"Yeah. I'll just have to come back tomorrow and restring it." He didn't want to alarm her until he found out how it had happened.

They returned to the ATV. He revved up and rode along the fence for a few meters before returning to the path on the east. After, they crossed to the west, and he showed her the other side of the property, ending at the main gate. He stopped to view the village from the road.

"I've been mostly in the house since I arrived," she said after looking on for a few minutes. "I didn't realize the property was like this."

Had she been sick the entire time or not in the mood to go out? He held off the questions, not wanting to pry, but still wondering about her.

He took the ATV up the main drive and parked by the large linden tree, the one bordering the old rose garden. He helped Catarina dismount, and she sat on the grass in the shade cast by the smaller trees around them. Afonso joined her.

Before them, the sun set lazily, casting orange rays along the golden shadows, and the breeze ruffled the leaves on the tree above. He'd arrived nearly two weeks ago, on a similar evening with just as stunning a sunset. Catarina was the first one he met here, and it had not been a good meeting. There was a tentative truce between them now, one that could easily progress into friendship. But did he really want a friendship with a woman? The last one had not ended so well. And to complicate matters, this woman was a recent widow, still recovering from her husband's death, still walking in a cloud of melancholy.

Already so much had changed. That terrible weight he'd been carrying for way too long had lifted, and he'd been too busy to notice how much lighter his heart had become. It was gradual, but it was happening, and maybe by the time he left Sunset Manor he'd be ready to try a new life without a vestige of the old one.

"This is a great tree," Catarina said after a stretch of silence.

He looked up in the same direction she did, under the wide canopy. "It has the perfect shape."

"When I was little, we spent summers at my grandparents' farm. My Romano grandparents." Catarina pulled her knees up and wrapped her arms around them." There was an oak tree in the backyard, and one summer Avô António hung a swing from the lowest branch." She looked to the branches with a pensive expression. "It became my favorite spot."

66

He could almost see a little girl swinging on the wooden seat, hair flying and carefree, unburdened from the worries of life. She wore those worries too much, in stern frowns and guarded expressions. This was the most relaxed he'd seen her yet. What would she look like with a genuine smile on her face?

As she lost herself in her memories, Afonso watched her. Her cheeks had a rosy tone to them, and her eyes shone in the warm evening light. She looked different today.

"Are you feeling better?"

Her expression turned serious, and her eyebrows knit together. "Feeling better about what?"

Maybe he shouldn't have asked. "From your sickness. You were in bad shape." It had been scary to find her like that.

She looked straight ahead. "I am feeling better. I've been careful to eat and drink regularly so I don't go through that again." After a pause, she added, "Thank you for what you did for me that day. How did you know I had to go to the hospital?"

This time Afonso broke the eye contact. "I have training as an emergency first responder."

"Is that what you did aboard the ship?"

He nodded. "Among other things. On a small river cruise ship, the only one who doesn't have double duty is the captain. Everyone else has more than just one responsibility." He'd enjoyed having different things to do every day.

"What kind of a captain is Matias?"

"He's just and honest, and the passengers love him. He also knows how to keep his crew working with a smile, even amid problems. Not an easy feat."

"Did you like working on a river cruise ship? Are you going back to it?"

She'd turned the conversation back to him.

"I liked it, but I'm done with that life. I was fired from the Gold River Company and no other river cruise company will ever hire me with my record."

"What will you be doing then?"

He shrugged. "I don't know yet." Did it matter what he did as long as it was honest work? "Something will come up."

"How long are you staying for?"

"Until the end of October. That will give me the time to finish all the projects before the winter comes. I'll have to ask Filipe when he's planning to return."

She lifted a shoulder. "I don't think he knows. He's talked about keeping the house, then he changed his mind and said he was selling it, then he changed his mind again."

"Where will you go if he sells the manor?"

She turned to look away from him. "I—I haven't thought about it."

Her expression closed off again. Her tolerance for questions of a more private nature was as low as before. Maybe he should wait to ask her another time, but his curiosity wouldn't let go. "Who's Juan-Carlos?"

Her face paled. "Juan-Carlos?"

Her Spanish accent was impeccable. She was back to repeating what he said, which she did when she got nervous. Maybe she did it to buy herself some time.

"You mentioned that name when you were sick. Was that your husband?"

Catarina sucked in a breath and pressed her fingers to her lips.

What kind of fool was he? "I'm sorry. I'm an idiot. I shouldn't have mentioned it." She was still very much affected by her husband's passing. "You don't have to say anything."

She nodded and looked away to compose herself, and he gave her a few minutes.

Afonso stood and extended his hand to her. They watched each other for a long moment before she finally placed her fingers in his.

Such a small hand she had. A need came over him to cradle her hand and protect her from the grief. But it was not up to him to console her.

They mounted the ATV without saying anything else, and Afonso drove it around the house to the back. She didn't put her arms around him this time, and he maneuvered slowly so she could keep her balance.

At the kitchen door, she hesitated before entering, then turned to him. "Thanks for showing me the grounds."

"You're welcome."

She stood silent but didn't rush inside either.

"I'm going to return the ATV to the barn, and then I'll be a while. I need to make a list for my shopping trip on Friday."

She straightened her posture. "Where are you going shopping?"

"Some supply stores in Castelo Branco. Do you need anything?"

"I need to run some errands in the city. Can I get a ride?"

"Sure."

After she entered the manor, Afonso had second thoughts about her coming along, but it would be rude to take back the offer.

He'd have to keep the questions to himself and the conversation to neutral themes. As long as he remembered to stay away from getting too personal, it would be okay.

CHAPTER SIX

$\mathcal{C}$atarina woke to phantom sounds of distant music in a fading dream. The melody wasn't distinct, but it sounded like a piano.

Outside the windows, the sun hadn't risen yet. The soft pink glow of morning had begun dissipating the last grays of night. It was too early to be up, and she was now too awake to return to sleep.

In her dream, she'd been dancing with Afonso. She was dressed in the pink kimono, and he wore only a bath towel around his waist, and they twirled and twirled around the music room to the three-quarter beat of a waltz. Were crazy dreams another pregnancy symptom?

She stretched in bed as she thought of the day before, of seeing Afonso in that towel and nothing else, of grabbing on to him on the ATV for the grounds' tour, of sitting with him under a linden tree at sunset. When was the last time she'd sat with a man and just talked? During her time dating Juan-Carlos, he'd provided opportunities for long conversations and quiet, romantic moments. The Rosy Period, as she called it, had lasted a few months into their marriage, enough to make her feel secure before Juan-Carlos had started showing his true colors.

Afonso hadn't fabricated the quiet moments; they'd just happened naturally. He'd taken all her questions in stride, answering all of them without hesitation, without seeming to mind her probing and curiosity.

She hadn't reciprocated. She couldn't. And when he'd asked her about Juan-Carlos, she'd let him think she was too emotional about the recent passing of her husband, instead of upset at herself for letting Juan-Carlos' name slip. What kind of widow was she who didn't mourn her husband? A liar, for sure.

What if Afonso recognized the name? What if he found out who she truly was? He could make a seemingly innocuous comment to Senhor Francisco, who would then say something to his wife, and Dona Madalena was the busybody kind. Before long, the whole village would know Catarina was staying at Sunset Manor, and if someone took a picture of her, they'd recognize her as Dulce Vega, the late Juan-Carlos Aragón y Vega's missing wife. From there the word would leak out to the media, and throngs of journalists would descend on the property looking for a scoop.

She didn't want to be accosted by paparazzi again. The days between Juan-Carlos' accident and funeral had been terrible as the paparazzi had followed her everywhere, invaded her privacy, and printed lie after lie for the whole world to read. No, she didn't want to go through that ever again.

Sharing anything too personal with Afonso was out of the question. Let him think she still grieved for a husband who had only wanted her in his life for the convenience of having a young, agreeable wife who looked good on his arm.

Why had she stayed with Juan-Carlos for seven years?

Catarina blew out a breath and pushed her thoughts away.

It was all in the past. She would never go back to that life.

And she wouldn't say anything to Afonso, no matter how patient and kind he was, and how good he looked without a shirt on.

After making a trip to the bathroom and drinking a tall glass of water, she sat on the bed, listening. It wasn't a dream. Someone was playing the piano somewhere in the house. Someone could only be Afonso. Why was he playing at five in the morning? She hadn't noticed a central sound system, so he must have his own speakers.

She reached a hand out to the pink kimono but stopped midair. Maybe it was a bit absurd, but her dream was still too vivid in her mind.

Instead, she pulled on a pair of purple yoga pants and a black tunic and tied her hair in a low ponytail.

The sound increased as she descended the stairs. When she reached the ground floor, she had no doubt the melody was coming from the music room.

The door was barely closed, as if he'd been in too much of a hurry to make sure the latch had locked.

With a soft nudge, it opened noiselessly.

An empty room greeted her, as it had the few times she'd been there. Filipe hadn't furnished it. Nothing besides the old grand piano in the corner, its cover pulled onto the floor beneath.

Afonso sat on the bench, playing something vaguely familiar, his hands caressing the keys, his fingers running without hesitation.

She slipped through the ajar door and sat on the floor, leaning against the wall and making herself small so he wouldn't notice her presence. He faced the other way, his back to her, and as long as he didn't turn, he wouldn't see her.

This moment—she didn't want it to stop. She closed her eyes and let the notes fill her heart. With joy and happiness and a sense of peace she couldn't remember having in a long time.

During the years she'd been married to Juan-Carlos, they'd attended concerts and recitals, both in Barcelona and in Lisbon. Juan-Carlos had fancied himself a patron of the arts, even if hobnobbing with celebrities and royals had been more important to him than the programs or the musicians.

Afonso had no pretense. Nothing seemed to matter to him than the music.

She lost track of time. The hard wall and uncomfortable floor didn't matter, and she could have stayed in the same spot for hours, listening to Afonso.

As another melody crescendoed into the next movement, he hit a dissonant key and stopped. He played the last few notes again, ending with the same off-key sound. Then he ran through a series of upper and lower scales and arpeggios, rapidly at first, giving in to a slower rhythm, and hitting specific keys as he played along.

To her untrained ear, some of the notes didn't sound as clear and melodic as the others, but Afonso seemed to know exactly which ones they were.

He stopped at last, ran a hand through his hair, and blew out a breath. He closed the lid onto the keyboard and stood, then reached for the cover on the floor. When he straightened, his eyes landed on her, and he stilled.

"Catarina." He slowly rose, absently holding on to a corner of the cover. "How long have you been there?"

Her legs had cramped up, and she stretched them out before standing. "A few minutes." Maybe longer. She couldn't remember.

Afonso finished covering the piano and crossed the room to her. "I didn't mean to wake you."

"You didn't." Not directly. Dream-Afonso had more to do with waking her up than real-Afonso. "You're a pianist?" Of course he was. She'd just heard him. Couldn't she think of anything smarter to ask?

He held the door open for her, and she passed through.

"I was, but not anymore." He looked at her. "You're dressed already. Aren't you going back to bed?" He gestured at the closest window. "The sun is not even up yet. Would you like to join me for breakfast?"

She followed him to the kitchen. "Okay." Did she even want to eat breakfast this early? In any case, she wanted to talk to Afonso and find out how he played so well.

Within a few minutes, Afonso had fried eggs and ham with sliced tomatoes on a platter. "I lived in London for a season and got used to the British breakfasts. Minus the baked beans and sausages."

Catarina eyed the food. She hadn't taken the anti-nausea pill, but maybe she'd be able to keep it down. As she took small bites, Afonso poured orange juice into a glass and drew a bowl of sliced strawberries from the refrigerator.

"Did you play professionally in London?"

"With the Royal Philharmonic as part of a cultural exchange."

"Where else did you play?"

Afonso finished chewing and set his fork down, as if giving himself time to come up with a reply.

"I'm being too nosy, aren't I?"

He smiled a lazy half smile, his eyes locked on her, and her cheeks heated. "I don't mind. To answer your question, I played in London, Lisbon, Barcelona, and Berlin for a few years. Then I got tired of the touring and applied with the Gold River Company."

"You were the pianist on board."

He nodded. "I liked the change of pace and the lack of stress that was always present in professional performing. Playing on board was more fun."

"Why do you say you're not a pianist anymore? You're so talented."

He wrinkled his brow and chuckled. "That piano is so out of tune, it sounded like a drowning cat."

"And still you played it better than a lot of musicians do."

He finished eating and sat back, watching her with a depth that drew her in and wrung her out as if he understood what lay beneath her mask. His gaze was steady, full of unspoken questions that she wasn't ready to answer.

Catarina hurried on to say something to distract him. "It's not the first time you played the piano since your arrival, is it?"

He blew out a breath. "I tried to stay away but…" A shrug lifted his shoulder.

"You probably didn't get a chance to play while you were … uh, inside," she said.

"You mean prison. You can say it. It doesn't bother me talking about it." He balled the paper napkin and dropped it on the plate. "No pianos there, that's for sure."

Afonso took the plates to the sink, and she followed with the glasses. "Why were you playing so early? You don't have to hide it from me. Or do you prefer to play with no one around?"

"I wasn't trying to hide it. It was the only free time I had before I go out for the day." He stacked the rest of the dishes and picked up the rag to wipe off the counter.

Catarina extended her hand. "I'll finish cleaning up the kitchen. You can go."

He held on to the rag. "Are you sure?"

"Maybe I can't cook, but I can wipe a counter." It had been a while, but how hard could it be?

As she reached for the rag in his palm, Afonso squeezed her fingers before passing it on to her.

"Thanks, Catarina."

He left out the back door, and she stood by the sink without knowing what to say in response.

Every day he did something that took her by surprise. She was running out of excuses to keep his friendship away.

How many things could go wrong in one week?

Apparently every day, sometimes more. Falling in the bog on Monday had been the least of his problems. He'd also found the wires cut in the north pasture when taking Catarina for a tour of the grounds. She'd actually been the one to point it out to him, since he'd been so focused on her body pressed to his back. On Wednesday the right back tire on the Ford truck had a nail he'd failed to see. Locating a spare and taking the tire to the village to be fixed had taken longer that he'd predicted. A whole afternoon wasted.

As Thursday rolled around, Afonso tried to push away his irritation. Senhor Francisco and Dona Madalena had returned from their minivacation while he'd been in the village.

He wanted more private moments with Catarina like the ones he'd had during the Silvas' absence.

It was wrong to wish for time alone with her. Having the Silvas around made it easier to avoid problems. There was nothing going on between him and Catarina, and feeling like he had a right to wish for it was entirely inappropriate. He should be glad the Silvas were back.

When Senhor Francisco paused for a lunch break and invited him to come along, Afonso declined. They'd been working in the northeast field where a series of ruts and bogs had crossed from the other side of the fence onto the property. After going back for his camera to take pictures of the evidence, Afonso had leveled an area close to the front of the house and had brought in the extra dirt on the ATV's trailer. They weren't finished yet.

He paused and leaned on the shovel's handle. "I think I'll pass. I gotta finish this today."

Senhor Francisco removed his hat and mopped his forehead. "Do you want me to bring you a sandwich or something?"

He wasn't hungry, but he didn't want to be rude. "That will work. Thanks."

The old man crossed the field until he reached the path, and Afonso turned to the small trailer to shovel more dirt.

Someone had cut the fence and rutted the field on purpose. He couldn't find any evidence of anything missing or any damage in the barn, the garage, or around the house, but this week he'd added daily inspections of the perimeter to his schedule. If the issues persisted, he'd contact Filipe about it, but for now he didn't want to alarm anyone unnecessarily.

Afonso worked until he ran out of dirt, but the ruts weren't filled yet, and he hopped on the ATV to get some more. He made a mental note to have some soil delivered to the property. As he started down the path, he found Catarina, a small basket in her arm, walking in his direction. He slowed as she reached the ATV.

"You didn't come in for lunch."

She wore a large frayed straw hat, one that had seen better days. He tipped his chin toward it, and she touched the brim.

"Dona Madalena lent it to me." She patted the handle on the basket. "And she sent lunch."

He cut the engine and dismounted. "I guess I can spare a few minutes." He couldn't, but it was too late for that. Missing lunch had been part of his plan to stay away from Catarina. Not because he didn't want to see her, but because he wanted to see her too much. It was better to keep his distance. And here she was.

They walked off the path and sat in the shade of a young chestnut tree. Catarina settled the basket on the ground between them and pulled off the cloth, uncovering the food inside: a cold meat sandwich on half a loaf of bread, an apple, and a small wedge of Gouda cheese. Water and beer bottles leaned together to one side.

Afonso unwrapped the sandwich. "Obrigado, Catarina."

She leaned back against the tree. "Dona Madalena had the idea and packed it. I just brought it."

"Thanks for bringing it." He smiled at her, and her expression relaxed. He'd make sure to go in for lunch tomorrow and save Catarina a hike through the field. Eating with the Silvas was less dangerous to his heart than sitting under a tree with Catarina. He could get used to it easily.

"I didn't think I'd like the landscape in this part of the country, but there's something about sitting under a tree, don't you think?" Catarina asked.

Afonso stilled, his sandwich midair. Hadn't he just been thinking the same thing? "How so?"

"It stops the busyness. It gives me time to slow down and think." She glanced at him.

He understood how she felt. "Every night on the river cruise, the ship docked at a different port, towns on the river banks. I played until after dinner, and then I had the rest of the night off. I'd find a quiet spot and watch the lights across the water. The landscape is different here, but the moments are similar."

Catarina nodded and let out a long sigh, her eyes landing on the scene before them—the house and the outbuildings, the row of linden trees sloping toward the road and beyond, to the village. He resumed eating his sandwich, his mind holding on to the words between them.

She cleared her throat. "How's the work going?"

Was she trying to make small talk? "Well. And you?"

Catarina scoffed lightly. "Not much to do around here. I'm dying of boredom."

"What do you like to do?" He phrased his question carefully, trying to find out more about her without tripping the alarms that would have her raise a wall immediately.

"I'm not sure." Her eyebrows wrinkled. "I'm trying to move on from what I did before." She glanced at him. "That's kind of vague, isn't it?"

"I understand. I feel the same way." He held his hands up and turned them, exposing the calluses and scratches crisscrossing his skin. "The work here is different, more physically demanding. But I like using my hands this way. It makes me feel like I'm accomplishing something."

Catarina raised her fingers as if to touch his palm but dropped them to her lap instead. "Do you think you'll ever go back to playing the piano profession-ally?"

"I don't think I will, but who knows? I've learned not to make long-term plans. Life can get at you real quick. But if the right chance comes along…" Afonso finished eating the cheese and slipped the apple in his pocket for later.

"I wanted to be an interior decorator when I was in high school," Catarina said quickly. She took a breath and then chuckled lightly, her cheeks flushing at the outburst. "I even helped my Tia Antónia, who had an interior decorating workshop."

Afonso took advantage of it. "What did you like about it?" he offered her the first sip of cold beer but she shook her head.

"Going into a room and seeing the possibilities." She waved her hands as she talked. "Finding the right pieces that work with the light and the space, and with the owner's personality. The colors, the textures. There's so much that goes into it."

His chest expanded at her excitement, and he smiled. "I bet you have lots of ideas for Sunset Manor."

"This place is a dream canvas." Her face lit up. "If I had my sketchbook and pencils, I'd start planning the rooms."

"You should talk to Filipe about it."

Her eyebrow rose. "Maybe I will."

When they drove to Castelo Branco, Afonso would add a trip to the art store to his list of errands.

CHAPTER SEVEN

*W*hen Catarina arrived on the front steps of the house, Afonso opened the passenger side door to her and smiled. "Bom dia," he said to her.

"Bom dia," she replied with a smile, climbing in.

He wore jeans and a dark gray T-shirt, and she watched him as he went around the truck. His hair had begun to curl around his ears and at the back of his neck, and the light scruff on his face looked good on him. Juan-Carlos had shaved every day, sometimes twice a day, but she liked to see Afonso with a three-day beard.

He climbed in behind the wheel. "Where do I need to drop you off?"

"Downtown will be fine."

Afonso had errands to run in Castelo Branco, supplies to pick up, and she was riding along for her first doctor's appointment with one of the obstetricians recommend by the ER doctor.

Nerves filled her chest, and she clasped her hands in her lap. Even though the ER doctor had confirmed her pregnancy, this was her first official appointment. According to what she'd read online, she should have had the first one at eight weeks. But back then she hadn't been emotionally equipped to deal with the realities of a pregnancy, let alone schedule doctor appointments.

Worry surged through her. What kind of mother was she, unable to provide for the baby she carried? Filipe was generous, but she couldn't live at his expense for the rest of her life.

She blew out a breath. One thing at a time.

They arrived in Castelo Branco, and Afonso wound his way to the town's center.

"It's not a very big town, is it?" The town was decidedly provincial, surrounded by villages, fields, and hills dotted with farms.

"It's a good size for this part of the country. About fifty-six thousand inhabitants by the last census." He stopped at a red light and turned to her. "Have you not been here before?"

"If you don't count the hospital stay, no." Filipe had picked her up in Lisbon and driven her straight to the house, where she'd been since arriving. Sightseeing had been the furthest thing from her mind.

The town was picturesque: red roofs and historical buildings, edging up the hill to the ancient castle for which the town was probably named. On a much smaller scale, it shared a similar silhouette to Lisbon, and Catarina found herself paying attention to the public buildings. What kind of opportunities were available in this part of the country? How long would she have to stay in the district?

He pulled the truck in front of a public park. "I'm going to need two or three hours to pick up the supplies."

Catarina grabbed the door handle. "That's perfect. I'll meet you here then."

Afonso's hand landed on her wrist. "Wait. Do you still have my phone number?"

Her eyes shot to his fingers wrapped around her forearm. When she looked back up at him, Afonso didn't immediately remove his hand from her. The contact seared her and raised the hairs on her arm at the same time. Fire and ice.

He released her slowly, and Catarina clasped her purse. "I—" Her voice faltered, and she cleared her throat. "I have your number."

"If you get done early, let me know." His expression was gentle.

A car behind them honked twice, and Catarina nodded then quickly exited the truck. Afonso merged back into traffic, and she watched him go until the vehicle disappeared down the street.

She stood on the sidewalk for another moment. Was it all in her mind, or was she physically reacting more and more to Afonso's presence? Whenever they spent time alone, there was something between them, something she didn't want to qualify or think about for too long. Something she longed to have for more than a moment.

The doctor's office was located in the newer part of town, a twenty-minute walk away. After confirming the route on her phone, she shouldered her purse and set walking in that direction.

She arrived with time to spare and filled out the registration papers using her maiden name, grateful her Portuguese ID was up-to-date. Her Spanish card would have given her identity away.

By the time the nurse practitioner finally called her name, Catarina's anxiety had doubled. For as many blog entries and online articles she'd read, reality was so much different than expectation, and reading about things that happened to other women wasn't the same. Today was about her.

The nurse had Catarina stand on a scale, took her blood pressure and a vial of blood for testing, and handed her a small cup with a lid.

When the doctor came, Catarina had been waiting for almost half an hour.

"Hi, I'm Dr. Paula." The doctor was a woman in her early thirties with short hair.

Catarina hid a sigh of relief. A female doctor would be so much easier to deal with.

Dr. Paula consulted the tablet she carried. "Catarina, right? I see this is your first pregnancy. Congratulations. Your blood and urine test results are all fine. Do you remember the first day of your last menstrual period?"

She shook her head. "My periods have been irregular for a while."

"That's okay. We'll get your baby measured with an ultrasound."

An ultrasound that would show her the baby. Was Catarina even ready for that? Did she want to know the baby's gender? There were so many things for her to consider that she hadn't yet.

"How long do I have to wait for the ultrasound?"

"One to two weeks, depending on the scheduling availability. We don't do those here at the office. The secretary can help you schedule it." Dr. Paula made an annotation on Catarina's file. "Based on your hCG levels, you should be eighteen weeks along."

Catarina's eyes widened. "Eighteen weeks?"

"Does that surprise you?"

"I didn't think I was that far ahead." Almost halfway done with her pregnancy. How was that possible?

The doctor stood. "Let's take some measurements."

Catarina lay down. Prone and flat on her back, the bump was more noticeable than in an upright position.

Dr. Paula frowned. "You're measuring quite small. Have the measurements been consistent? How much did you weigh before you got pregnant?"

Catarina hesitated. Juan-Carlos had been insistent she keep her weight right under fifty kilograms, but she'd probably weighed less when she arrived at Sunset Manor. With the morning sickness and irregular meals, she must have lost weight since then. "I think it was fifty kilos."

The doctor frowned. "Have you had any problems?"

She had plenty of problems but none she wanted to talk about. "I had nausea and vomiting."

"Which is normal. But if you've lost weight, it could be cause for concern. You can't afford to lose any more weight. You're too small already. You have been taking your prenatal vitamins, right? Do you need a new prescription?"

Catarina could answer truthfully to that. "I've been taking them at night, and I could use a new prescription." She'd fill it at a pharmacy before she met with Afonso.

Dr. Paula swiped a page on Catarina's file. "Do you have a supportive environment at home?"

Catarina hesitated. A few weeks ago, after Filipe left, she would have said no. But Afonso was supportive, even if he didn't know she was pregnant. "Yes, I have help at home."

Dr. Paula brought out a device that resembled an old microphone and pressed it to Catarina's belly.

A fast rhythmic thump-thump, thump-thump filled the room from the small speaker.

"That's your baby's heartbeat, Catarina," the doctor said with a smile.

Catarina held her breath. The baby she'd wanted for so many years was real. Nothing made it more real than hearing that heartbeat coming from her belly. A tear rolled down the side of her face, and she wiped it. "Oh my goodness," she said after a moment. "There really is a baby in there."

Dr. Paula chuckled. "Of course there is."

Catarina smiled through her tears. She was going to be a mother. Already she was a mother, as proved by the sweet little sound of her baby's heartbeat. "It's so fast and loud."

Dr. Paula put the device away and helped her sit up. "Just as it's supposed to be, fast and strong. Have you felt your baby move?"

"I don't think so." Catarina reached for a tissue and dabbed her eyes.

"First-time moms sometimes have a hard time identifying the baby's movements. But since you're measuring so small, it could be you're carrying your baby toward your back, which would make it harder to feel. Let's see you back here after the ultrasound for a quick visit."

The receptionist helped Catarina schedule an ultrasound at the imaging center and booked an appointment for the same day.

Catarina found a nearby pharmacy and bought a new box of prenatal vitamins. As she walked back downtown to meet with Afonso, she passed a shopping area with storefronts. The white-on-blue Chicco logo with the red dot stood out to her, and, before she could talk herself out of it, Catarina went in.

Had she thought yet about everything a baby needed? She walked around the store looking at items she didn't even know existed, let alone knew were necessary. The prices shocked her. Ironic that she never would have thought twice about paying €200 for an infant carseat when she'd been married to Juan-Carlos, but now that she needed to buy baby gear, she couldn't afford any of it.

She'd have to research what was absolutely indispensable. It would be easy to get carried away and buy beautiful, unnecessary baby items that she couldn't afford. Did she even own anything that she could turn into cash? If she could find a buyer for the diamond studs, she'd try selling them, but she had no idea how to go about it.

"Can I help you find anything?" the store clerk said.

Catarina put the soft blanket back on the shelf and resisted pulling the sunglasses onto her face. "I—I don't know what I'm looking for." This was a mistake; she should have never come in.

"Is it for a gift?" the clerk asked.

"Yes," Catarina replied quickly. "It's for a friend due next month, but she doesn't know the gender of the baby." Why did lies come so easy? Guilt pricked at her as she thought of Afonso and his unflinching honesty.

Her chest tightened, and sweat beaded at the nape of her neck. Catarina hadn't intended to get anything, but she couldn't resist the idea of buying a keepsake for the baby, something small that could be easily kept from view. Other than the doctors, nobody else knew she was expecting, nobody else celebrated the existence of this unplanned, surprise baby. What kind of mother was she if she didn't celebrate? She took a breath, a surge of emotion rising in her chest.

When the clerk steered Catarina to a display of brightly colored stuffed toys, Catarina reached for the lion.

"This one is a musical toy. It plays Brahms' lullaby when you pull on the cord." The clerk demonstrated. The melody was familiar, but Catarina couldn't place it.

"I'll take it."

The clerk wrapped it, and Catarina paid for it, the anxiety mounting as each minute passed. Once on the sidewalk, she stuffed the small bundle in the pharmacy bag, grateful it fit well enough to hide from sight.

As she resumed her walk, she slowed her pace and took a deep breath. Then she realized what she'd bought: a musical toy that played Brahms' lullaby.

She'd been thinking of the Brahms' waltzes Afonso had played on the piano. The melodies had stuck with her and now she had bought something that unconsciously reminded her of him.

Not Juan-Carlos, her late husband and the baby's father, but Afonso, the groundskeeper she'd met a few weeks earlier.

Would Afonso even be around when the baby came?

If Filipe decided to sell the property, she would be living somewhere else as well.

Afonso parked the truck at a nearby public garage and walked to where he'd dropped off Catarina earlier. It had taken him longer to fit what he could in the truck bed and order the larger supplies to be delivered, including a load of soil.

Catarina sat on a park bench under a wisteria tree. When the breeze blew, the purple petals scattered around her, and she swept them off her lap.

The pink tunic she wore brought out the rosy tone in her cheeks. Her face had filled out a bit, and she had a healthy glow, but it was hard to tell how much weight she'd put on with the large clothes she wore. It was almost as if she hid herself in ill-fitting clothing and behind large sunglasses. What would it feel like to hold her in his arms?

The thought stopped him cold. When did he start wishing to hold Catarina? He couldn't entertain such thoughts.

"Sorry I'm late." He sat next to her. "I hope you haven't been waiting for long."

"Not too long." A relaxed smiled graced her expression. "It's nice here in the shade.

"Did you do everything you needed to?"

She crossed her hands over the purse and pulled it onto her lap. "Yes. Thank you for the ride. I'm ready to go."

He stretched an arm over the back of the bench,

angling his body toward her. "There's a school supply shop not too far from here that carries art materials. Afterward we could have lunch. If you're not in a hurry." As much work as he had waiting for him at Sunset Manor, taking a break for lunch sounded better than clearing overgrown bushes. Besides, Catarina hadn't been in town before.

"What kind of art supplies do you need?"

"A sketch pad and some pencils. Can you help me choose?"

She frowned, a little wrinkle between her eyes he hadn't notice before making an appearance. "Wait a minute. Are those for me?"

Afonso chuckled. "You caught on to that, did you?"

Her face bloomed into a smile. "I should say no to the art supplies, but I'm not going to."

"Good," he said. A stray petal was tangled in her hair, and Afonso reached for it. Her breath hitched, and she stilled as his hand hovered near her face. He held her gaze and for a crazy moment imagined what it would be like to lean in and kiss her. Catarina scooted back, and Afonso came to his senses and did the same. He must have been loading the truck in the sun for too long. Kissing her was a bad idea.

He cleared his throat. "For lunch we could grab some sandwiches and eat at the gardens of the Episcopal Palace." As long as he kept it to lunch only instead of staring at her lips.

Forty-five minutes later they entered the gardens and found a stone bench in the shade by the staircase that led to the upper level. Afonso had never visited Castelo Branco before coming to Sunset Manor, and his brief excursions since then had not given him the time for any sightseeing. If he was honest with himself, he just wanted to prolong his time with Catarina before returning to work. He knew he shouldn't, but he couldn't resist being in her company. As badly as they'd started off when he'd arrived at the manor, his attraction to her grew every time he saw her and with every conversation they had. And last night, she'd come to him in his dreams, a sign that his mind was at peace. He couldn't remember a dream in months, certainly not while he was in prison. Dreaming of Catarina at night and spending time with her during the day didn't help his resolve to keep his distance.

For all they'd talked about, Afonso still didn't know much about Catarina. She shared childhood memories but didn't talk about her recent past, and certainly not about her husband, his last name, or what had happened to him.

Was Afonso making the same mistakes he'd made with Anabela? Getting close to a woman who didn't open up as he did with her?

Catarina was different from Anabela. She didn't manipulate him into doing things that only benefited her, but she still had secrets, and he couldn't go down that path again. This pull he felt toward her—he'd put a stop to it. If he kept away from her, he'd safeguard his heart.

After they ate, they walked through the gardens, as he'd promised Catarina, but he cut the tour short. Despite her obvious confusion, she didn't ask for an explanation, which only made Afonso feel worse. Anabela had always wanted to know why he did everything, whether it concerned her or not. How could he have been so blind to her scheming and manipulation?

His phone vibrated with an incoming message. **Can we talk?**

He frowned. The number was one he didn't recognize. He slipped the phone back into his pocket.

"Do you need to send a reply?" Catarina asked.

"No, it's probably a wrong number." He shouldn't have had the phone out in the first place.

The drive back was quiet for both of them. His thoughts distracted him, and the woman sitting beside him intrigued him too much. Catarina seemed preoccupied with something, probably related to whatever she'd done in town.

As they approached the village, a full-size van behind them honked the horn twice. It was larger than the Ford pickup and Afonso could discern two passengers in the front—a man and a woman wearing sunglasses. He slowed down to let them pass, and they slowed down too. The road only had two lanes but there was enough room for the vehicle to pass. Why didn't they do it?

Afonso kept an eye on them in the rearview mirror.

Catarina glanced over her shoulder. "Is there a problem?"

He didn't reply right away, keeping watch.

"Afonso, you're all tense. What's going on?"

"I'm not sure. I thought they wanted to pass, but they pulled back." The other driver slowed down and turned into one of the neighboring farms.

Afonso relaxed his grip on the wheel and kept a steady speed.

A few minutes later, the same van appeared on his rearview mirror, gaining speed. It accelerated until it came on behind the truck, barely missing it.

Afonso turned on the blinkers to pull onto the shoulder, and the van accelerated again, but instead of passing, it rode up next to Afonso. Afonso hit the horn and the other driver hit his back.

"What are they doing?" Catarina's voice pitched higher.

"I don't know, but I'm trying to pull over."

When he glanced over to the other vehicle, the woman in the passenger seat turned to Afonso and smiled.

He knew that smile. It chilled him. Afonso's heart dropped in his chest. How was it possible that she'd found him?

In the second it took him to get his focus back, the van sideswiped them off the road.

Catarina screamed.

"Hang on!" he said to her.

He grabbed the wheel and held on to it, easing into the brake until the Ford came to a stop in a ditch, leaning forward at a slight angle.

With the heavy load in the back, he'd feared they'd overturn, but he'd managed to prevent it.

He turned to Catarina. "Are you okay?"

She nodded, breathing hard.

Afonso released his seatbelt, hopped out and opened the passenger side door. "Can you get out?"

"I think so." Her voice trembled, and the click of the seat belt followed.

He was ready to catch her, and his hands went around her waist, setting her down on the ground. Her knees buckled, and he brought her up against him with a firm hand against her back. Catarina sighed and relaxed in his arms for a moment. Afonso released a pent-up breath, grateful nothing worse had happened; mad at the other driver for putting them in danger.

When Catarina let go of him, Afonso led her to a grassy patch, and she sat down. "Are you sure you're okay? You don't have any injuries?"

"I didn't get hurt. Just a bit shaken." She looked to the truck, pitching forward in the ditch, doors wide open. "Who were those people?"

"I don't know the driver, but I think I might have recognized the passenger."

He drew out his phone from his front pocket. After locating Matias Romano's number, he hesitated for a second before calling him.

He answered right away. "This is Matias. Hello?"

"Captain Romano, it's Afonso Cortez. I'm sorry to be calling you." He didn't know if the captain was on duty.

"You're fine. It's my off week. What's going on?"

"Have you had any updates on the case, sir?"

Catarina remained seated, watching him tiredly with questions in her eyes. Afonso offered her a half smile. How could he reassure her when he had so many doubts?

"Not in a while. Last time I talked to Senhor Valadares, the investigator still didn't have any leads. Has something happened?"

"I think I have a lead." He wasn't sure, but who else could it be?

"Where are you?"

"I'm still in Castelo Branco. Well, we're near Sete Fontes, the village on the way to your cousin's property. A passenger van forced us off the road, and we ended up in a ditch. I didn't recognize the driver, but I think the passenger was Anabela."

"Are you sure?" Matias Romano's voice took on a more urgent tone.

"She wore sunglasses, and the driver sped off after hitting us. I was trying to keep us upright and didn't even get a good look at the license plate."

"There wasn't one," Catarina said in a low voice.

"Is someone with you?"

"Yes. I'm actually here with—"

Catarina stood and tugged on his arm, shaking her head. Her panicked expression stopped him. "I'm with a friend, sir."

"Just call me Matias. Did you or your friend get hurt? Was there any damage?"

"We're fine. No damage." He placed a hand on Catarina's shoulder, and she breathed in deeply. "I'm just mad at the situation. Especially if it is her. I'm sorry I can't be more certain." It was too much of a coincidence.

"I think you did well in calling me. We can't be too careful where it concerns Anabela Rialto." Matias said something in a hushed tone to someone else. "I'll call Senhor Valadares and apprise him of the situation. Let me know if anything else comes up."

"I will."

"Afonso? Be careful, and take care of your friend too."

Afonso hung up. Catarina had sat back down, with her legs pulled up and her chin resting on her knees. He joined her on the ground, and she turned to look at him.

"I have so many questions, but I'm tired. Can we go home?"

"Let me see if I can get the truck out of the ditch without help." He turned his palm up, and she took it.

Catarina wasn't the only one who had questions.

CHAPTER EIGHT

$\mathscr{A}$s soon as Afonso stopped the truck in front of the garage, Catarina jumped out and ran to the house.

"Catarina!" he called after her, but she didn't slow down.

She was furious with him. Her anger burned so hot she wanted to slap him.

Instead of driving straight home after getting the truck out of the ditch, Afonso had driven to Sete Fontes to file a police report. She'd tried telling him she didn't want to talk to the policeman on duty, but Afonso didn't listen to her, and they'd spent over an hour in a hot, cramped room while the village cop, clearly due for retirement, had typed their statements with only two fingers. The water bottles the policeman had given them were lukewarm, and the bathrooms hadn't been updated since the eighties, if not before.

But worse than all that was the chance of being recognized by the village people who'd seen them enter and exit the building. What if some of them had taken pictures?

Catarina ran up the staircase with Afonso right behind her.

"Catarina, wait." He caught up to her at the landing. "Please. I just want to talk to you."

She whirled around to him. "Why, Afonso? Why do you want to talk to me?" She crossed her arms.

"I just want to tell you—"

"Why should I listen to you? You didn't let me tell you anything back in Sete Fontes." Her voice rose, and she took a breath. "You wouldn't listen to me."

"I'm sorry, but we had to stay until the report was done. I know it was inconvenient and you were tired—"

Catarina took a step forward. "Tired? Do you think this is about me being tired?"

"You said the bathrooms were—"

"I can't be seen in public. Why can't you understand that?"

"This is the first time I'm hearing about it." He passed a hand through his hair. "You haven't told me anything, Catarina. Why don't you want Matias to know you're here? I've been trying to understand you, and you won't let me be your friend. How am I supposed to know what you need if you won't talk to me?"

"You're so stubborn, you know that?" Catarina clenched her fists.

Afonso stepped closer to her. "Now I'm stubborn? Because I care about your safety?" His voice lowered. "Or because I care about you?"

His words made her pause, and she looked at the man in front of her. "Why would you care about my safety?" She didn't dare repeat his last question. How could he care about her?

"Did you not hear a word I said?" He made a sound, almost a growl, deep with frustration and something else she couldn't begin to guess.

Afonso shot his arm behind her neck and pulled her close, his other hand splayed against her back, firm and possessive.

Catarina gasped, and his mouth landed on hers— fast, hot, insistent. She grabbed his upper arms and opened her lips to him, giving back with the same resolve.

Afonso was kissing her. He was kissing her.

She lost track of time as silent stars exploded within her, around her, inside her. All the stars she never knew could come from only a kiss. Afonso brought her closer still, and his kiss evolved into something deeper and sweeter. Catarina held on to him, wishing the closeness could last forever.

At last they broke the kiss, gasping for air. Afonso's hands slipped around her waist and he rested his forehead against hers. "Catarina..."

Afonso had kissed her, and she'd kissed him back with fierceness and heat. How could she call that a kiss? It was so much more. Was this the beginning of a relationship that had never even crossed her mind?

Catarina pulled away, unable to deal with all the emotions she saw mirrored in Afonso's eyes. "Can we talk later, please?"

Afonso nodded, and she took refuge in her room.

He'd kissed her.

After dreaming and daydreaming and fantasizing about kissing Catarina, after promising himself he'd never give in to it, Afonso had kissed her.

And not just any kind of kiss. For a moment, he'd let go of his control and drunk her in, tasted her as if he meant so much more with that kiss.

And it scared him that he did. He'd wanted her that much. He still did.

He was halfway to falling in love with Catarina Romano, and he didn't even know how it had happened. How could he have let his guard down?

He was the biggest idiot he'd ever heard of.

Afonso watched her, the click of the lock echoing through the empty hallway. The message could not be any more clear: she didn't want him. Why would she?

She was still mourning her husband, and Afonso had taken a kiss without asking.

He turned and went back outside, where he'd left the truck running and the doors still open.

Senhor Francisco approached and gestured to the Ford. "I turned the engine off."

Afonso nodded. "Obrigado, Senhor Francisco." Afonso pulled the key from the ignition and went to the back of the truck.

Senhor Francisco met him and started pulling out the supplies from the other side. "Everything okay?" He tipped his chin toward the manor house.

Afonso gave him a tight smile. "Yeah, it'll be okay." Nothing was okay, but what else could he say?

They worked side by side until they'd stacked the supplies in the barn, and Afonso placed all his misspent energy into the mindless task.

When he was done, he turned to the older man. "Some people from my past might be coming around." As much as he didn't want to alarm the Silvas, he had to warn them about the situation.

Senhor Francisco leaned against the open barn door. "Would this be a good thing?"

Afonso shook his head. "No, this would not be a good thing."

"What do they look like?"

"A woman in her early thirties. She might have a man with her. I saw them driving a passenger van, but they could be driving something else too. She's pretty, with dark blonde hair, and she can talk you into anything."

"You say that from experience?"

"That I do, unfortunately." If only he could turn back time and undo his mistakes.

Senhor Francisco nodded. "A pretty snake."

"The worst kind."

"I'll have to tell my wife."

"Please do."

Afonso took the ATV and rode the perimeter of the property, making sure nothing else had happened since his last inspection. He drove out to the main gate and checked the wall and the fence from the outside.

When he reached the top of the road, he stopped to watch the late sun graze Sete Fontes as the day waned before him. Up here, peace and solitude were a possibility, something he could easily attain if he stopped caring about everything else.

Afonso had wished for Sunset Manor to be an island away from his former life and from the reality of the rest of the world, but islands were not fortresses, and a pretend life wasn't much of a life at all. Sunset Manor had been Plan A, the regroup-and-start-over plan. But he should have learned by now that plans didn't work, and unwittingly a Plan B had taken over, the fall-in-love-and-mess-everything-up plan. Did he dare think Catarina might be his Plan C?

He could still feel Catarina's lips on his, the way she'd trembled under his touch. He unclenched his hands and blew out a breath.

He'd been mad at her for calling him stubborn when she was the stubborn one. After all the promises he'd made himself to keep away, it hadn't taken much to give in.

How was he going to forget that kiss and pretend it hadn't happened?

How could he begin to convince Catarina she could trust him?

On the way back to the barn, he stopped at the linden tree where they'd sat before.

Afonso looked up to Catarina's bedroom and thought he saw her retreat away from view.

Gaining her trust was going to take a lot more than a conversation, especially when she didn't want to talk to him.

He looked back to the tree. It did have the perfect branch for a swing.

CHAPTER NINE

*E*very night in her dreams Afonso came to her and kissed her. Those kisses had the same passion and fervor she remembered, but the frustration mounted when she woke each morning.

She knew what the real kiss was like, and dream-Afonso's kiss was not the same as the one she'd received from real-Afonso.

They still hadn't talked. Afonso had tried, and although a man who wanted to discuss his feelings was a new experience for her, she'd been avoiding that conversation. Unless talking about a kiss brought another kiss, what was the point of it? It was too complicated. She craved simplicity. The simpler the better.

Through the ajar door, the far-away sound of the piano reached her ears. Only in the early morning when everything else was quiet could Catarina discern the music with a few off-key tones. Afonso played every day now; or maybe he'd played every day before and she'd never heard it. Now she was more in tune with him, and his notes came more easily to her, bringing a peace and calm she'd never expected.

How frustrating was it to play on a broken piano? Could it even be fixed? Did he wish for a newer one with unstained keys and a perfect tone? She was like that—stained and imperfect.

Catarina pushed at the sheets and stretched her arms and legs. Another restless night, another night of wishing for what she could not have.

Afonso had kissed her, but he didn't know about her. He would never want her once he found out the truth. Why would he?

She was pregnant with another man's child, a penniless widow who'd lost everything. She was a liar who kept secrets about her own identity and about her past. She didn't deserve happy endings.

Nobody would ever want her again. Least of all Afonso.

Her hands slid to her belly. As her fingers cradled her small, round stomach, the flutter of a butterfly grazed from the inside. Catarina stilled. Was that the baby moving? How could she know for sure? Tears swamped her eyes, and she brushed them off with an impatient hand.

There was no one to share the moment with her.

Catarina rolled to the side and curved into a ball.

Hours later, when she woke again, the sun was high and the light bright. Since coming to Sunset Manor, where none of the windows had curtains, her body had learned to sleep without room-darkening blinds.

A knock sounded at the door, and Dona Madalena pocked her head in. "May I come in?" She carried a tray in her hands.

Catarina sat up in bed. "What time is it?"

Dona Madalena placed the tray on the chair and sat on the edge of the bed. "It's way past noon. Senhor Afonso said to let you sleep in and to bring lunch up to you."

Catarina's cheeks heated. "Oh, I wish you hadn't. You'll think I'm lazy." Her stomach rumbled at the sight of food. She spooned the scrambled egg onto the corner of a piece of toast and took a bite.

"Rest and nutrition are a sign you're taking care of yourself. And taking care of yourself means you're caring for the baby too."

Catarina stilled. "What did you say?"

The older woman smiled and drew the box of pre-natal vitamins from her apron's pocket. "You left this downstairs. Did I assume too much?"

A sense of relief came over Catarina that someone else knew her secret. "No, you're right. I am pregnant." Catarina took the box and placed it under her pillow. "Did anyone else see it?"

"Men are easily distracted, and they don't need to know what doesn't concern them." She winked at Catarina. "Besides, it's not my secret to tell."

Catarina took a drink of milk and set the glass down on the tray. "It's not the kind of secret I can hide for much longer. Everyone will know pretty soon."

"I think you'll find out that this kind of issue has a tendency to resolve itself." Dona Madalena stood from the bed. "I'll come for the tray later." She gestured at the closest window. "You should open up the window. It's a beautiful day today."

Catarina ate everything Dona Madalena had brought: the scrambled eggs, the toast, the yogurt and mixed berries. She'd gained an appetite in the last few days and with the nausea gone, she was eating more than she could remember before. Was eating for two a mental excuse, or was there some truth to it?

The sky was the bluest she'd seen in a long time. She approached the window and pulled up on the sash, letting the fresh air and the birdsongs in. If her life were a musical, this was the moment where she'd open her mouth and sing. The thought brought a smile to her lips. Even if everything wasn't going perfectly, she still had reasons to be grateful for what she did have. A speck of hope took hold in her heart, however brief and light it was.

A movement by the largest linden tree caught her eye. Hanging from a branch, a swing swayed gently in the noonday breeze. From her bedroom window, it looked to have a wooden seat, but the rest of the details were hard to make out in the distance. She frowned. What was Afonso up to?

When Catarina brought the tray to the kitchen, Dona Madalena turned from the sink and smiled wide at her. "Did you see it? What do you think?"

Catarina sat down on the closest chair. "Do you mean the swing? Did Afonso get it?"

"He didn't get it. He made it. With my Francisco's help." She rinsed a small pot. "But Senhor Afonso did all the work, looking for the best wood, finding out which kind of rope wouldn't give splinters. You should have seen the planning he did. And today he got up at sunrise to hang it from the tree. He took his time with that. And then he called me to make sure it was level and swung straight, but I told him the person who the swing is for should be the first one to ride it."

"You're saying he made the swing himself?" Catarina asked.

Dona Madalena wiped her hands on a kitchen towel. "That he did. Did you go try it out yet?"

"No, I didn't."

"He put so much work into it. It'll be a shame if you don't."

"I'll go later, when the sun is lower." She wasn't ready to see the swing or Afonso. "When is he coming for lunch?"

"He came by for a quick sandwich only. My Francisco stayed for a full lunch, but I couldn't convince Senhor Afonso to sit at the table. He said he was too busy."

He was too busy to sit for lunch, but he'd spent hours making her a swing. Catarina tried to understand his motivations. Juan-Carlos had always wanted something in return when he did something for her.

The Silvas and Catarina were in the middle of dinner when Afonso came in through the service door.

He poked his head in the kitchen. "Don't wait up for me. I'm going to take a shower and get some laundry done."

He'd started keeping a change of clothes in the laundry room, most likely to avoid being seen wearing a towel and nothing else. Probably for the best, even if Catarina had enjoyed the view that one time. She chastised herself and shook the mental picture. With her luck, it would come back to haunt her dreams again.

When dinner was done, Dona Madalena dragged Catarina to the front of the house and out the main door. "Come on, Menina Catarina. I want to see you try that swing before we leave tonight." The Silvas returned to the caretaker house every night, a ten minute walk to the east side of the property.

She'd been battling curiosity all day, telling herself she didn't want to the see the swing.

But she did. Nobody had ever made her anything, not since second grade when Avô António had made wooden toys for all the grandchildren for Christmas. Juan-Carlos had preferred the convenience of what money could buy. There had been many expensive gifts over their married years, but not anything that he'd put more effort into than handing over his credit card. There she was, throwing comparisons again.

Dona Madalena and Catarina arrived at the tree, and Catarina stopped to admire the swing. It had been sanded smooth and varnished to a polished coat, enhancing the color of the veins in the wood.

"It's chestnut," Dona Madalena said. "He found it on the west side."

Catarina touched the seat. "What do you mean?"

"He didn't buy the wood. He found a felled tree, and he had it cut in the village. Then he spent a week sanding it by hand into the perfect shape."

"How do you know all this?"

"Senhor Afonso asked my Francisco for help."

The rope had been encased in transparent tubing, a good way to avoid splinters.

"Have a seat already." Dona Madalena propelled Catarina closer.

Catarina sat down, and her hands wound around the rope. It surprised her how wide the seat was, comfortable and deep. She wouldn't be slipping off this one.

How many years had it been since she'd been on a swing? Probably the summer when she was sixteen. She'd sneaked a few times when the older cousins weren't looking and the younger ones were too busy with something else. In her seventeenth summer she'd gone to the Algarve with some friends to work there, and a year later she'd married Juan-Carlos a week after turning eighteen.

If only she could go back and undo some of the bad decisions she'd made. If only it were that simple.

After Dona Madalena left with her husband, Catarina stayed on the swing, pushing her foot against the
ground, back and forth, back and forth. The gentle
rhythm soothed her, and as the bright sun faded into
pink ribbons against the sky, Catarina let go of her
worries, if only for tonight.

She placed a hand on her belly. "It's you and me,
baby. Just you and me."

When she heard the front door open and close, she
didn't have to turn to know it was Afonso. Maybe it
was time she stopped running from him.

Afonso leaned against the tree a few paces away
from her, watching the sunset. "I hoped you'd like
it," he said softly.

Catarina slowed down but didn't stop the swinging. "I like it. Obrigada." She met his eyes and gave
him a slow smile.

His hair was still wet from the shower, and he'd
changed into the jeans that looked too good on him
and the soft-from-wear blue T-shirt that brought out
his chocolate eyes.

"De nada." He bent down and plucked a blade of
grass between his fingers. "That was one of the few
things you've shared about yourself."

She'd barely shared anything personal, and he'd
remembered. "I just don't understand why you did it."

"Can't friends do things for each other?"

Catarina almost paused the swinging but kept
going, not wanting to change anything in the moment
around them.

A friend. Afonso Cortez called himself her friend. Catarina's chest filled with a strange emotion, and she wanted to close her eyes and peer at the feeling more closely. But doing so would call Afonso's attention to her, and he was already watching her so attentively.

He locked his eyes on her. "I'm sorry for the way I handled the situation at Sete Fontes." He passed a hand through his hair, as she'd noticed him doing when he was nervous and frustrated. "I freaked out when we were forced off the road. Not for myself, but for putting you in danger." He looked away and then back at her. "I don't know what she wants or why she's come back, but I can't stand that you were caught in it."

Catarina stopped pushing her foot and turned to Afonso. "Who is she?"

"Her name is Anabela Rialto. She's the one who sabotaged the *Princess Catarina*, putting everyone's lives in danger." Afonso scoffed. "And I protected her by not telling anyone what she was doing."

After the sun went down, they moved to the library. Catarina sat on the leather sofa, and Afonso took the chair closest to it. Did she think he was the dumbest man alive? He already knew he was, but he cared about her opinion, and he fiercely wished she could see how much he regretted his past, how willing he was to change his future.

"Why did she do it?"

He shrugged. "She lied to me, so who knows?" Anabela had lied to everybody. "I'm sure she had her motivations and, in her mind, she probably thought she was justified, but her gross disregard for safety and physical property prove she only cared for herself."

"Were there any injuries?" Catarina's expression showed interest and concern, not disgust, and Afonso's hope rose a notch that she wouldn't think ill of him.

"Only minor ones, thank goodness, but the repair costs totaled thousands of euros." His indictment had included a report of the damage.

"And you think she was the one who pushed us off the road?"

"A man was driving, but she was the passenger." His jaw clenched at the memory.

"Has she tried to contact you?" Catarina settled against the corner and crisscrossed her legs. "What do you think she wants?" Her expression was open and her eyes laden with concern, encouraging him to go on.

"I don't know." He rubbed the back of his neck where a tension knot had taken up residence in the past few weeks. "I did get a text that same afternoon when we were in Castelo Branco that could have been from her, but I have since bought a new phone and changed service providers so that won't be happening again." If Anabela wanted to talk to him, she'd have to do it in person.

"I shouldn't have forced you to go to the police station without telling you my plans. But I wanted to remember all the details and get a report out since there's a warrant for her arrest." He let out a long breath. "It still doesn't excuse the way I dismissed you. I'm sorry."

He remembered the frustration as well. For a week after the accident, he'd been in close contact with Matias and Filipe, reporting back to them after his patrols on the perimeter while trying to keep the regular schedule. Despite being on alert, he hadn't seen anyone or anything unusual. He drove to the village every other day, and even once to Castelo Branco to pick up more supplies, but he hadn't seen Anabela again, nor the vehicle. As a precaution, Afonso had ordered digital security cameras that he could check remotely on his phone and tablet, and after picking them up in Castelo Branco, he'd spent two early mornings installing them around the exterior of the manor before Catarina got up for the day.

Catarina had kept to her bedroom during that week and only came to the kitchen when the Silvas were present as well. Had that kiss meant anything to her? He couldn't get it out of his mind. After unsuccessful attempts to talk to her, Afonso started planning the swing. At least it partially worked—she was asking him questions.

Maybe he could try asking her one too. "Why can't you be seen in public?"

121

Catarina winced and turned her face away from him.

If she had a hard time trusting him, how was he supposed to protect her? "Do you believe I'd bring any harm to you, Catarina?"

She sighed heavily. "No, of course not."

He waited, but she didn't say anything more. After a long minute, he added, "You know where to find me when you're ready." He rose from the chair. He didn't like forcing her to talk to him, but how else would he find out what she needed?

Talking to Catarina was useless, especially when she didn't say anything. What he needed was work. He should have started pruning the rosebushes weeks ago. A pair of pruning shears would do the job.

"Afonso, wait." She followed him. "I came to Sunset Manor to hide," she started.

He had guessed as much. Afonso took a seat on the sofa and waited.

Catarina joined him. "There was—there was a scandal surrounding my husband's death." She drew her knees up and looked at her toes for a moment.

She wore a summer dress, something flowy and suncolored, with spaghetti straps that wouldn't stay put. Afonso's hand itched to bring the thin band to its rightful place and brush his fingertips across her skin. The extra weight looked good on her, had filled some of her curves, and he longed to have her in his arms again. Kissing her once had not been enough.

"The paparazzi hounded me." Her mouth formed a thin line. "It got really bad. Filipe saw it on the news and came for me, brought me here. The media thinks I'm in Spain, and I'd rather nobody finds out my location."

The questions came to Afonso one after another, but voicing them would only make her raise the barrier she hid behind. He settled for one question. "Why don't you want your family to know you're here?"

Her shoulders dropped, and her spine bowed. "I broke my ties with them when I left." Catarina's voice lowered. "I met Juan-Carlos when I went to Spain with a friend after we graduated from high school. My friend and I were supposed to work for the summer and start college in September, but when Juan-Carlos proposed, I didn't care about any of that anymore. When I called my parents and told them, they said I should come home. Instead I eloped." She sighed, her eyes still down. "I made so many mistakes. It's better if they don't know where I am."

He didn't agree with her decision, but it wasn't his place to say anything on the subject. Her confessions were vague but the most she'd told him about her situation. It was a start. "I repeat what I said, Catarina. You can trust me."

The corners of her mouth raised in a smile, but it didn't extend to her eyes. "Obrigada, Afonso."

"I've noticed you like to stick to the manor."

She ducked with a sheepish look in her eyes. "I guess I'm a bit paranoid, but I can't risk being seen. I just want a chance at a clean start. Is that too much to ask?"

"No, it's not."

That was what he wanted too. Maybe she wasn't as hard to understand as he'd thought.

He cleared his throat. "Are we going to pretend we didn't kiss?"

"Is there any point in talking about it?" She traced the pattern on the blanket draped over the armrest. Her cheeks flushed, and she kept her eyes down as if it were the most interesting thing she'd seen all day.

She couldn't even face him. Regret surfaced inside him again. "I want to apologize to you. I shouldn't have kissed you. It was wrong of me." He shouldn't have brought it up either.

Catarina looked up at him. "Wrong? What do you mean?" Her eyes flashed at him, dark with an emotion he couldn't decipher.

This time he was the one who couldn't look at her, for the shame he felt. "Your husband hasn't been dead for too long, and I'm sure you miss him a lot. You have more to think about than me forcing a kiss on you." It had been a heck of a kiss and as much as he'd like a repeat, he'd do well to stay away from her and forget the attraction. She needed the time to move on, and she'd have as much time as she needed. He wouldn't be interfering with it.

Catarina put a hand up. "Stop, Afonso. Just stop. You're assuming too much about me, and that never ends well. I—" She sighed. "I really don't want us to fight." The weariness in her voice cut him.

How much was he assuming of her? The questions came, but he swallowed them. This wasn't about him. It wasn't meant to be.

CHAPTER TEN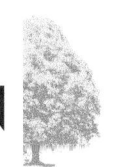

$\mathcal{A}$fonso poked his head in the kitchen and looked around. Dona Madalena stood at the stove and smiled when she saw him. "If you're looking for Menina Catarina, she's in the library."

Afonso carried the roses to the sink. "Good. It'll give me time to get these ready." He opened the cabinet doors nearby. "Do you know if there are any vases in the house?"

"I don't think we have any, but there are some glass jars and glasses that might work." She opened another cabinet door to show him.

"Perfect. Obrigado, Dona Madalena."

The roses from the garden didn't have the long stems of store-bought roses. Instead, he'd strip the leaves and place them in small bunches in the short glasses, in the same style of what he'd seen in the dining room of the *Princess Catarina*. He picked three tumblers and brought them to the sink.

While Dona Madalena finished the preparation for the weekend meals, Afonso worked on the flowers, removing the thorns and leaves and grouping the roses in assorted colors. When he was done, he had enough flowers to arrange in three glasses.

He took one and carried it to the library. He pushed the door open and called her name. "Catarina?"

"In here."

She sat on a chair behind the door, exactly situated in the corner of the room, with the sketch pad and the pencils on her lap.

Her hair was pulled up in a high ponytail and she wore the green tunic that made her eyes pop. The tension between him and Catarina had lightened after last evening's conversation. Maybe not everything was resolved, but the way she'd opened up to him had forged a tentative trust between them.

His lips parted, and he took a step toward her. "The first roses from the rose garden." He held up the vase. "Well, not the first ones that bloomed, but the first ones I picked." Now that he'd pruned and fertilized the rose garden, the roses would come in better quality.

Catarina's face lit. She placed the pad and pencils on the chair and rose to meet him, then took the vase in her hands. "They're so pretty." She brought the flowers up and inhaled. "And so fragrant. Obrigada."

"You're welcome." He had to distract himself before he leaned in and kissed her. "How's the sketching doing?"

She picked up the pad and angled it his way. "I took the measurements, and I'm working on the room's perspective from each corner. It's only a rough draft."

She'd drawn the library from the open door looking in. Filipe's desk and the leather sofa and chairs were rearranged differently and the bookcase displayed rows of books.

He looked up and gestured at the bookcase. "Filipe mentioned the books were in storage. Maybe we should find out where and get them in here."

Her eyes widened. "Would you ask him? That would help make the room so much cozier and lived-in." She paused for a moment. "I took your advice. I called Filipe and asked him if I can sketch the rooms and show him a decorating proposal, and he said yes."

As much as he wanted to hug her, Afonso raised his palm for a high five. "That's great, Catarina. This house has been empty and naked long enough."

She raised an eyebrow. "Have you been talking to Filipe? That's exactly what he said."

Afonso smiled. "What else do you have planned for this room? Do you go to furniture stores for ideas?"

"Sometimes I look at magazines or online, and other times I find a piece and know it will work out for what the space needs. But this is the first time where I'm actually starting from scratch and on such a scale. I worked with Tia Antónia and sketched individual rooms, but this—" She turned around and encompassed the room with her arms. "This is epic.

I'm really excited about the music room and turning the piano into a focal point."

"That piano needs a lot of work." The old piano was a relic, probably dating back to the last century.

"Do you think a piano tuner would be able to fix the sound?"

"Unless it's missing keys or the damage is more extensive than it appears, a good piano tuner could take care of the adjustments to make it sound well again. The wood casing needs some attention too."

"You mean the wood parts on the outside of it? What kind of attention?"

"A new coat of polish for sure. I haven't taken a serious look to see if it needs sanding and filling in the small cracks with putty. It's a great piece, notwithstanding its age. I actually like playing old pianos. The aged wood gives a different sound. And I don't mean the off-key kind." He chuckled. "I'm glad you're taking this on."

The smile on her face widened, and Afonso found himself grinning back, caught up in her enthusiasm. "It looks good on you."

She raised an eyebrow. "What does?"

"Joy. Happiness. Whatever you want to call it. You just look happier in the past few weeks, and it's a good change."

Her lips parted in a breath, and she watched him. "You always say the nicest things to me."

His chest warmed, and the need to take her in his arms came at him out of nowhere. Afonso slipped his

130

hands in his pockets and stepped away, not trusting himself. "I need to finish a few more things before I call it a day. I'll see you later."

He turned to the door, but she called after him. "I have a favor to ask. The Silvas are giving me a ride to Castelo Branco after lunch on Friday, but I'll need a ride back later in the afternoon."

"Sure. Just send me a text."

She thanked him but didn't move. "This is embarrassing to admit, but I never learned how to drive."

"Nothing to be ashamed of. Things happen. And you can take driving lessons anytime."

"I need someone to drive me," she said quickly, her cheeks turning red. "I joined a group on Facebook that posts about antique sales and flea markets in the area."

Catarina needed a driver. That's where she was going with her confession. "If you can wait until next Saturday, I can drive you into town. We'll make a day of it. Will that work?"

She nodded. "That would be great. Obrigada."

Was it possible that her smile could affect him even more than before?

After another awkward moment, Afonso said goodbye and walked to the kitchen.

He'd just offered to spend more time with Catarina.

Oh, sweet torture.

After using lined paper and a school pencil, Catarina couldn't get enough of the sketch pad and professional pencils. Afonso's thoughtful gift was as wonderful as the man himself, and she couldn't help a smile every time she caught details on the paper.

Guilt pinched at her for a moment. When Afonso had talked to her, she'd purposefully let him believe he was right in his assumption that she needed the time to mourn. In his words, she missed her husband.

Nothing could be further from the truth.

It weighed on her. The subterfuge. The lies. The carefully hidden half-truths. What would Afonso say if he knew all the facts?

She brushed the thought aside and concentrated on the paper on her lap and the pencil in her hand. The clean, straight lines of the rectangular dining room with its tall, even windows and lofty ceilings afforded her the perfect perspective as she got more familiar with each space at Sunset Manor. Online, she curated furniture pieces onto virtual pinboards, where she could pretend to have a budget and access to everything she needed. It would come soon. She was confident Filipe would agree to her proposal.

The drawing and design classes she'd taken in high school hadn't been enough. After pestering Tia Antónia for weeks, her aunt had finally relented in taking Catarina as a sort of apprentice in her interior decorating workshop. Catarina had also watched shows on the Home Decorating Network and even though she'd lacked the funds for decoration projects, she'd rearranged the furniture in her family's apartment, much to her brothers' irritation.

After marrying Juan-Carlos, Catarina had given up her dreams of going to interior design school. Another regret in her life. How hard would it be to enroll in college in Castelo Branco? Would she even be able to attend part-time? She'd need a job to support herself and her baby. Whatever money was left from Juan-Carlos' investments, if there was any at all, would be tied in legal proceedings for years.

The ride to Castelo Branco with the Silvas seemed longer than usual. Dona Madalena chatted the whole time, excited to meet with one of their sons and grandchildren. They dropped her off downtown, and Catarina walked to the imaging center, her anxiety building with each step she took.

When the technician called her, Catarina hurried from her seat in the corner. Her heart beat with nerves and excitement, her emotions split and swirling, her body cold and hot.

"Catarina, my name is Fernanda." The technician guided Catarina to the exam table in a semidark room. "You're here for your twenty-week ultrasound, is that right?"

Catarina nodded as she reclined, her hands balled at her sides.

"Can you please verify your full name and birth date?"

Catarina recited the information.

When the technician's hand touched Catarina's arm, Catarina startled.

"Are you a little nervous?" Fernanda rubbed Catarina's arm and smiled. "Let's get started and take a look at your baby."

The technician reached for two small sheets, and Catarina pulled up her tunic to expose her belly.

"Look at the cute little bump you got there," Fernanda said as she tucked the sheets around the top and the bottom of Catarina's belly.

The technician dispensed some lubricant onto Catarina's skin and followed with the ultrasound wand. Catarina craned her neck to look at the screen, trying to decipher the images as they formed.

"This is the head, and this is your baby's spine." Fernanda explained.

As the dark images started to make sense for Catarina, warmth radiated from her chest, the emotion swelling and expanding until lightness replaced the former worry. She swallowed, letting a small tear run down the side of her face, exhaling the tension from her body.

There was a baby inside her—a little person with a little body, formed perfectly and already moving around.

She'd waited so many years for Juan-Carlos to agree to a baby. Every year, her yearning had grown stronger, and every year he said no, never changing his mind. When she found out she was pregnant, she didn't know how to react, what to think. Other than confusion and uncertainty, and myriad feelings she'd tried to ignore for too long—she hadn't been prepared for the love that filled her heart, the wave of love that coursed through her. A smile stretched her mouth.

"Look, your baby stuck his thumb in his mouth," Fernanda said.

Catarina smiled. "Is it a boy?"

"Just a manner of speech. I didn't look yet. Do you want to know the baby's gender?"

Catarina stuttered. "Uh—I don't know." She hadn't even thought about it. "I think I'll wait to find out." She wasn't ready to find out the gender. Maybe she'd wait until the birth.

The technician kept a running commentary, taking measurements and recording them. At the end of the appointment, she pushed a button, and the machine printed a strip of pictures. "Your baby's first pictures." She helped Catarina into a seated position and then handed the photos to Catarina with a smile. "I'll send the report to your doctor."

The medical office was close by, but an hour later Catarina sat in the examining room still waiting.

At last, Dr. Paula breezed in. "Catarina, I got the preliminary report from the ultrasound, and your baby looks great, just a little small. Let's take your measurements again."

Catarina lay down, and Dr. Paula stretched the measuring tape across her belly. "You're still measuring small as well, but the growth is consistent with the last measurements."

Catarina sat up. "Is that a problem?"

"I think we have a case of small mom and small baby. As long as you're eating healthy, taking your vitamins, and resting properly, I don't see cause for concern. You probably won't need maternity clothes for a while," she said, gesturing to the elastic band holding the button on Catarina's pants.

Catarina wasn't in a rush to wear maternity clothes.

Dr. Paula patted Catarina's hand. "I'd like to see you in four weeks."

After leaving, Catarina walked to a nearby city park and found a bench tucked away in a corner. She retrieved her cell phone and held it in her hand for a moment. She wanted to call Afonso and tell him about the ultrasound, tell him about the baby. He was her friend, and the need to share with him something that brought her so much happiness filled her chest. But how would he react? While his friendship was increasingly becoming more important to her, her baby superseded it.

Her shoulders dropped. Instead of calling, she typed a short message. **I should be done by five.**

His reply came immediately. **Where do you want me to pick you up?**

Same place as before is fine.

When she put the phone back in her purse, her fingers brushed the small box, the one she'd found at the bottom of the wardrobe. She kept the box inside the purse and peeked inside. The pair of diamond studs caught the light and winked back at her, and next to them rested the platinum wedding band Juan-Carlos had given her on their wedding day. She'd been wearing both the earrings and the band when Filipe brought her to Sunset Manor, and they were all she had left from the jewelry Juan-Carlos had gifted her over the years.

There were a few pawn shops in Castelo Branco, and she'd entered the locations on her phone. Would she be able to get a fair price for the pieces? After her appointment with Dr. Paula, Catarina would walk to all the shops, if need be.

She needed the money too much.

CHAPTER ELEVEN

*A*fter seeing the sketches for the music room and the dining room, Filipe had called Catarina and asked her to start the plans for the interior decorating for the whole house. In the next month, a tentative routine took root between Catarina and Afonso.

On Tuesdays, Wednesdays, and Thursdays, Senhor Francisco helped Afonso on common projects. On Mondays and Fridays, Afonso worked other tasks by himself.

Catarina became familiar with the house and its architectural qualities. The way the sun bathed the building throughout the day intrigued her, and she sketched various versions of each room on the ground floor and upstairs until she filled the sketch pad with details from every angle.

On Saturdays, Afonso drove her to markets in nearby towns, in particular a warehouse where she found most of her favorite pieces. Little by little, the plans became more complete, and her vision for each room would soon be more than just on paper. Maybe she'd get the courage to ask Filipe for a recommendation as an interior designer when she moved out. In any case, Catarina took pictures of each room in its "before" look. The start of her portfolio.

The swing had become one of her favorite spots and often, after dinner, Afonso would follow her to the large linden tree, where they watched the late sun spread its colors in a languorous setting.

On Wednesday, Catarina had been working on the old piano for almost two days. With Afonso on the property and far from the house, she stole away to the music room and pulled the cover off the piano. Dona Madalena had brought old sheets to protect the floor and, after her last trip to Castelo Branco, Catarina finally had all the ingredients for the natural furniture polish: olive oil, lemon juice, and lemon essential oil, mixed well in a spray bottle. Flannel rags turned out to be the perfect cloth for the job, and she worked in small sections, alternating between standing and sitting, taking breaks to walk and unfold her legs. Maybe the homemade furniture polish was not as effective as the commercial kind, but, in her present condition, the natural recipe was safer, and promised results just as glossy.

The piano tuner was coming this morning, and the furniture from the warehouse would be delivered in the afternoon. The Ford truck had been too small for the largest pieces, and Catarina had hired a moving truck.

When a loud knock sounded at the front door, Catarina rushed to get it.

A man with cropped gray hair carrying a weathered leather bag stood on the steps. "I'm Abílio Moreira, the piano tuner. Is this the right place? Are you Catarina Romano?"

She opened the door wide and let him in. "Yes, I am. This way, please."

He walked with stooped shoulders, gazing around the entryway and admiring the skylight. "Fancy place you got here. I'm not feeling so bad about the travel fees."

Catarina was, but she didn't comment. Paying Senhor Moreira to come all the way from Coimbra to tune the piano was an expense that had taken her several days to justify. His travel fees alone cost almost as much as some people earned in a month. And those were people with jobs, people who actually earned money. She had neither a job nor a salary.

But she had Afonso. The thought snuck up on her. She had him as her friend, which was more than she could say of most anyone else for the past several years. Except for Filipe, who was family, and maybe felt some sort of duty toward her.

Afonso had been so kind and done so much for her. She wanted—needed—to do something in return. And so she'd managed to set aside enough of the precious euros from the sale of her jewelry to cover this one expense. The rest she would save toward the support of her baby.

Catarina wouldn't be living at Filipe's expense in the new year, maybe even before that. Not that he would kick her out, but she had a shred of pride left, however thin and feeble. Sacrificing her meager funds to do this one thing for Afonso meant more to her than all the expensive gifts she'd given Juan-Carlos. In her heart, she knew why, but Catarina pushed the feeling aside and concentrated on getting through the next few hours successfully.

"This is it." She swung the door open and walked ahead to retrieve the spray bottle and rag.

The man approached the piano and set down his bag. "I haven't seen one of these in a long time." His hand passed reverently over the wood. "Have you been polishing it? I hope you're spraying the cloth and not the wood directly."

"Yes, of course." She did know that much, thanks to Google.

The man knelt and opened his bag of instruments. "It'll take two hours, at least, if not more." He started immediately, propping open the piano's lid.

Catarina took her spray bottle and flannel rags and moved her polishing efforts to the banister on the grand staircase. It didn't need it, having recently been revarnished. She used a clean rag and buffed the dark wood. From this position, she'd be able to see anyone who came through the front door or from the kitchen. Maybe it was foolish to hope Afonso would like her surprise, and even more foolish to spend her own money on the tuning, but how could she not?

Dona Madalena talked Catarina into a mid-morning snack, and Catarina easily gave in. The old lady reminded Catarina of her Romano grandmother, Avó Teresa, with her concern and her advice. Just like Avó Teresa, Dona Madalena offered her opinion and counsel whether Catarina asked for it or not. But the voice of experience was hard to argue with, and Catarina had learned enough difficult lessons in the past few months to know when to listen, even when she hadn't asked.

An hour later, when Catarina took a bottle of water to the piano tuner, he called her over. "Do you see this sticker here?"

She leaned over to peek where he pointed. There was a name, a signature, and a date.

"It means this piano hasn't been tuned in twenty-five years. Good thing it's an instrument of quality." He waved her off. "I should be done in another hour."

When she returned, he'd began packing his tools. "Who's the pianist? You or your husband?"

"Definitely not me. It's a surprise for him." Why did everybody assume she had a husband? Didn't she look like she could be the independent type?

He rose, holding the bag. "I can guarantee you he'll be surprised." His hand rested on the wood. "It sounds better than new." The pride in his voice was hard to miss. "Too bad I can't stay to hear him play it." He followed Catarina to the entry hall. "Tell him to make sure it doesn't take another twenty-five years to tune it again."

Catarina drew the cash from her pocket and paid him the remainder of the fees. So much money. Had she done the right thing? Only the anticipation of seeing—and hearing—Afonso's reaction when he played gave her strength to know she wouldn't regret hiring the tuner. It would be worth it.

She went back to polishing the rest of the piano and left the cover off so the wood could dry.

When Dona Madalena came to get her for lunch, Catarina was ready for a break. She was looking forward to seeing Afonso, but he didn't come. Instead, Senhor Francisco asked his wife to pack two lunches, and he returned to the grounds.

Catarina took a short nap after lunch, and weird dreams plagued her sleep. When Dona Madalena knocked on her door an hour later, Catarina woke with a start.

"The delivery people are here. Do you want them to park at the front or at the back?"

"At the front, please."

She took a few minutes to comb her hair and brush her teeth, hoping the sleep wrinkles on her face weren't too noticeable.

When Catarina opened the front door, a woman with short hair stood on the steps. Behind her, at the back of the truck, two guys opened the latches to the double doors.

144

The woman held a clipboard in her hand. "I have a delivery for Catarina Romano."

"That's me."

"My name is Joana. I'm from the warehouse, and I'm here to ensure the delivery goes smoothly," the woman said. "This is such a large, expensive order, and I don't want anything to go wrong. Will you show me where the pieces go?"

She had a friendly voice and a no-nonsense attitude, and Catarina felt at ease.

Catarina unlatched the front door and opened both sides flat against the wall. As the woman walked into the entryway, her eyes widened. "This house is fantastic." Her admiration sounded in her voice.

Catarina opened the double doors to the dining room, then crossed the entry hall and did the same at the music room.

Joana turned to Catarina. "I can see you have excellent taste. The pieces you bought will really enhance these rooms."

Catarina hoped Filipe would share the opinion when he saw the transformation.

Joana showed the order list to Catarina, and Catarina indicated where each piece of furniture would go.

For the next hour, Joana closely supervised the men as they unloaded and brought in the pieces Catarina had bought on previous trips—a console and a pair of chairs for the entry hall, a pair of upholstered chairs and a rug for the music room, a dining room set composed of a table for sixteen people with fourteen straight chairs and two chairs with armrests, and a two-meter-high gilded mirror.

Catarina stood to the side as Joana made sure that every piece was installed to Catarina's wishes.

After the rug was unrolled in the music room, Catarina stepped back when they brought in the first chair. Some minutes later, the second chair came, and she directed the seating arrangement at an angle to the piano. The gilded mirror came last, anchored on the opposite wall. The chairs made the perfect place to sit while Afonso played. A wave of excitement rushed through her, and she could hardly wait to see his reaction when he found out the piano had been tuned.

Joana watched as Catarina brought in a pair of pillows she'd bought at another store. "I'm telling myself to keep my mouth shut, but I really can't."

"Excuse me?" Catarina asked.

"I've been looking for the perfect house to showcase some special pieces, and this is it." Joana nodded to herself as she looked around. "Is there any way I could come another day to photograph some furniture for a catalog we're working on?"

Catarina frowned. "I don't think it's a good idea." She couldn't risk having any photos taken in the house.

"I promise we'd only photograph select pieces and nothing else," Joana rushed to say. "And we'll compensate you for your time, of course."

The money would be nice. Any quantity would be an improvement on what Catarina had at the moment, especially after paying the piano tuner. "Would you be able to add the images to the deal?" Catarina's portfolio would benefit greatly from professional images of the decorating she'd done.

Joana didn't hesitate. "Absolutely. Do we have a deal then?"

Catarina should talk to Filipe first. Even though she was the one in charge of decorating, the house didn't belong to her. "I can't commit right now, but I promise to consider it seriously. It's a really good offer."

They walked to the entry hall. Outside in the driveway, the two men secured the latches on the now-empty truck.

Joana handed the clipboard to Catarina for her signature. "Is this your cell phone number?" Joana asked, pointing to the information at the top, and Catarina confirmed it. "I'll be in touch then. It was a pleasure meeting you, Catarina."

"You as well, Joana."

After the truck left, Catarina locked the double doors. She turned around and smiled.

In the entry hall, the console and chairs already looked at home. The candlesticks she'd bought last week would complete the vignette.

But it was the music room that had her heart racing with anticipation. Would Afonso like the changes she'd made?

Afonso entered the kitchen with Senhor Francisco. Dona Madalena and Catarina sat at the table, both of them leaning over the tablet.

He sat down and within minutes, Dona Madalena had dinner served to Afonso and her husband. They didn't wait to start. After the long day he'd had, he was famished. Several fence posts on the north end of the property had been down, and Senhor Francisco and Afonso had worked all day to fix them. He didn't have any security cameras in the area, but it might not be a bad idea to install a few around the perimeter. He couldn't shake the feeling that someone was testing his limits. Who else could it be than Anabela?

Catarina scooted her chair closer to him. "They had the furniture delivered today. All the large pieces we bought at the warehouse."

Her face radiated happiness, and Afonso slowed down to watch her. "How did it go? Are you happy?"

She smiled at him. "Very happy. I can't wait to show you."

Afonso smiled back, unable to stop himself. "I can't wait to see it."

Catarina chatted about the furniture and how nice the delivery people had been. Afonso couldn't remember seeing her this relaxed, and it warmed his heart to see her like this.

Once he was done eating, Afonso took his plate to the sink. "I'm taking a shower. I'll meet you back here in a few minutes."

Catarina nodded, then picked up the tablet and showed it again to Dona Madalena.

He took the stairs to his bedroom instead of showering in the utility room off the kitchen.

When he returned, Catarina sat alone at the table.

"Where are the Silvas?"

"Senhor Francisco was tired, and they left a little earlier. Dona Madalena left food in the refrigerator if we want a supper."

"Maybe later."

Catarina stood. "Are you ready to come see the furniture?"

"Absolutely." He followed her as she left the kitchen.

She rounded the staircase and stopped at the wall nearest to the dining room. "Do you remember the console?" She gestured with both hands. "What do you think?"

The piece fit as if it had been made for the space. "It looks great. And the candlesticks."

She smiled. "They go great together, don't they? I still need to find a mirror that will fit on the wall above the console." She approached, as if she could see it there already. "If I can't find one, I'll have to search for an old frame and have a mirror custom fit to it."

At the dining room, she swung open the double doors. "I have a lot to do in the dining room. But

I think this table definitely sets the tone. And I love how the chairs complement it."

Afonso approached the table and ran a hand over the top. "Did you clean it?"

"Just a dusting with a natural polish."

"I thought I could smell something different."

"Now just imagine a chandelier over the table. That will be my priority for my next shopping expedition."

"You've been busy, Catarina."

Her expression bloomed in a genuine smile. "You like it? Do you think Filipe will?"

"How can he not? You're doing such a great job."

"Wait till you see the music room." She skipped ahead of him across the hall and opened the double doors.

The upholstered chairs she'd bought at the warehouse sat at an angle to the piano, anchored by a colorful rug.

Catarina had taken the cover off the piano, and the lid was propped up. The wood surface shone clean.

Afonso walked to it and stroked the top. "You polished the piano too."

"I think a complete restoration would have been too much, but it looks a little better, doesn't it?" Her uncertain tone brought his eyes up to her.

"It looks great. A resurfacing job would have taken away some of its character."

She sat on the closest chair and tucked her feet to the side, leaning an elbow on the armrest. The seating arrangement was perfectly angled to the best advantage of someone watching the pianist.

Afonso chuckled. "Is that why you placed the chairs in this position?"

"The best seat in the house." She shifted eagerly like an excited child. "You should sit down and play something."

"Sim, senhora." He pulled out the piano bench and lifted the lid. His fingers hovered over the keys as he went through the repertoire in his mind, all the pieces he knew by heart. "It's kind of a cliché, but it's still one of my favorites." He flexed his fingers again. "Just keep in mind this piano doesn't sound the best."

"Are you stalling, Afonso?"

He absolutely was. Catarina had watched him play before, but this felt different and he couldn't even explain it.

After taking a breath, he played the first measure and immediately stopped, raising an eyebrow. "Catarina?"

A smile tugged at the corner of her lips in reply. He rushed through the next few measures only to confirm what he heard—the piano had been tuned. The rich, deep sound and perfect pitch proved it.

He moved his hands to his knees and turned to her. "You had a piano tuner come out here?"

"I did. Did I surprise you?"

"Very much. How did you arrange it?"

Her expression turned playful. "With a phone call. Please, go on. Was that 'Clair de Lune' you were playing?"

"Yes, it was." He resumed playing, appreciating the clarity and precision. How had Catarina paid for a tuner? He'd have to mention it to Filipe.

The look of delight on Catarina's face kept him playing for almost an hour. Of all his years playing in the professional circuit, all the grand concert halls and VIP guests he'd played for—it was here, in this simple, half-furnished room, and for a woman healing from emotional scars he didn't even know the depth of, that Afonso found himself at peace, pouring his soul into every note, hoping she could understand all the feeling each one carried.

From his heart to hers.

CHAPTER TWELVE

$\mathscr{A}$t her next doctor's appointment, almost twenty-five and a half weeks into her pregnancy, Catarina was still measuring small. But with the growth keeping consistent and the measurements within the projected curve, Dr. Paula told Catarina not to worry.

Catarina tried not to. As she left the medical office and took the elevator down, she thought how she'd been feeling better than she had in a long time—she was eating well, had enough energy to last a whole day with only one nap, and was sleeping as much as the baby let her. As for the baby, it was a little ball of energy, always active. If this was any indication of how it would be after his or her birth, Catarina would definitely have her work cut out for her with such a busy little one. A smile graced her lips at the anticipation of meeting her baby.

When she exited the elevator, a lady holding on to a little boy's hand stood on the other side. The boy pulled away and jumped inside the elevator, barely missing Catarina.

"Rui, you need to hold Mommy's hand," she scolded. She looked up at Catarina. "I apologize."

Catarina smiled and waved it off as the elevator door closed again.

The boy reminded her of her younger twin brothers. They'd been constantly trying to get away from mom.

In the next instant, a prick of guilt niggled at her. Her family. She was expecting her first child, and she hadn't told her parents and brothers yet. They'd be grandparents and uncles soon and had no idea about it. Should she wait until after the baby was born to tell them, or would they want to know now?

Deep down, she knew the answer to that question.

And she also knew that if she told her family, she'd need to tell Afonso as well.

How was she going to do that? At times, she almost wanted Afonso to look at her and see it, but she'd never given him any indication that she was pregnant, and he didn't have a reason to suspect it. Would he be mad that she'd hidden it from him this long?

Maybe tonight she could find a moment to tell him. Afonso was picking her up and taking her to dinner downtown. Maybe she could find the courage to tell him her secret.

"Catarina Romano, what a surprise," a voice said.

Catarina stilled. She'd been so distracted, she'd missed the woman at her side. The face was familiar, and Catarina gave her a pale smile.

"You probably don't remember me, but I delivered furniture to your house last week," the woman said expectantly.

"Joana," Catarina said as she placed the woman. "Yes, of course I remember. How are you?"

"I'm well, obrigada. Hope you're not feeling sick," Joana asked gesturing to the building behind them.

The three-story building exclusively housed medical offices."Just a regular check up. And you?"

"I'm early to meet my sister. Are you in a hurry?" Joana gestured to the coffee house across the street. "I was going inside for an iced tea, but it'll be a lot more fun with some company."

Catarina hesitated. She'd planned to meet Afonso for dinner, but that was in the early evening. She still had plenty of time to run some errands and do some shopping before then. She accepted the invitation.

They crossed the street and opted to sit inside to enjoy the air-conditioning. The end-of-July temperatures were merciless during the day.

When the iced teas and custard tarts arrived, Catarina tried to relax. The café was busy, but nobody appeared to be looking at her. More likely, people were just taking a respite from the hard summer day. She should stop worrying about anyone recognizing her.

Joana reached for a tablet in her purse. "I'm so glad I bumped into you. I got the digital proof for the catalog cover, and I'd love your opinion."

Catarina leaned forward, already curious. "I'm afraid I'm more experienced with interior design."

"And that's what the catalog will be about. Plus, you also have such great taste." Joana showed her three options she'd received from the digital designer.

They discussed the best colors and layouts for what Joana had in mind, and Catarina explained the why behind every opinion she shared.

It was flattering to Catarina to know someone valued her opinion as worthy of contribution. Maybe letting Joana bring the photographer to the house after it was decorated was exactly what Catarina needed to get her started in interior design.

Joana insisted on paying despite Catarina's protests. "You helped so much. It's the least I can do for taking your time," Joana said.

Catarina thanked her. "It was my pleasure. I enjoyed it." She really had. Both the company and the task.

They stood on the street in front of the café before parting ways.

"My sister has another appointment next month. Would you consider meeting with me again?" Joana asked.

"I actually have to be in town next month too." Catarina had another appointment with Dr. Paula already scheduled.

"That's perfect." Joana touched Catarina's hand, a wide smile on her face. "I'll text you a date to see if it works for you."

Catarina floated for the rest of the afternoon. Hope took root in her. Hope that she would be able to get a job doing something she loved, something she was good at; hope that a future for her and her baby was not impossible.

By the time she met Afonso for dinner, she was ready to include him in all the plans she had for the future. Catarina steeled herself as she approached him, her fingers tightening around the purse's handle. Why did he have to be so attractive? As if being kind and honest and hardworking weren't enough.

Why couldn't she have married someone like Afonso? But she didn't want someone *like* him. It was Afonso she wanted.

Her heart tripped at the thought, and Catarina bit her lip. When she reached him, he smiled at her and her nerves dissolved.

Afonso wore a dark pair of jeans and a blue button-down shirt with the sleeves rolled back. She loved that look on him. He leaned down and kissed her on the cheek. Her eyes fluttered shut. He smelled so good. Her fingers tingled, and her chest heated at the contact of his skin on hers, and she rested a hand on his upper arm for balance as her legs wobbled. The need to stay close to him overwhelmed her, and she swallowed the catch in her throat.

Afonso stepped back. "I missed you," he said slowly, keeping his gaze locked on her. His eyes darkened for a moment, and an electrical feeling buzzed between them, strong and bold.

Catarina knew exactly what he meant, for it felt like they'd been apart much longer than half a day.

Afonso took her hand in his, and they walked side by side.

The restaurant was quiet. It was too early for the dinner crowd on a Friday evening in late July. Most tourists and locals would come as the sun set, but she preferred the relative privacy of an empty room before they drove home.

The maître d' seated them at a corner table with a view of the castle on the hill. Afonso winked at her, and a swarm of butterflies rose in her stomach. Or maybe it was the baby protesting at her anxiety. Could he or she feel how nervous Catarina was to be next to Afonso? He sat to her left instead of across from her, far enough to give her space but close enough that she could feel his gaze on her, the warmth from his arm resting on the table only centimeters away from her.

Dinner was wonderful—delicious food, interesting conversation, and excellent company had Catarina immersed in the moment, her worries forgotten, her plans for the future no longer taking all the space in her head. She pushed away everything else and focused on the man at her side. Afonso placed his arm behind her chair, and she leaned toward him, giving in to the attraction and not caring that he could see it in her face, in her eyes.

She wanted him to know.

They lingered over dessert for her and an after-dinner espresso for him, delaying the moment when they had to leave and face reality again. In the secluded corner of this restaurant in downtown Castelo Branco, Catarina had found a moment she wanted to hold forever, a little piece of magic. The pull between them was palpable, even more so because she saw it mirrored in Afonso.

"I'm not ready to go home just yet," Afonso said to her in a low voice.

"I'm not either." She could only agree with him.

He tipped his chin toward the window. "Have you been to the castle yet? I hear it has great views of the city."

"We should go see how great those views are."

"Let's go then."

As long as they were together, she'd go with him anywhere.

He was the worst kind of cad.

Catarina was attracted to him. Afonso could see it plainly in her eyes. For a few moments, she'd dropped her guard and he'd run with it, responding with his own attraction for her in little gestures that wouldn't spook her. Short of saying any words that would only make it more obvious, he turned all his attention to her, wishing they could be someplace alone, knowing it was better they weren't.

After leaving the restaurant, they drove to the bottom of the hill where they left the car, then walked the rest of the way to the castle. Afonso held on to her hand tightly, and when they reached the summit, they stopped at a parapet away from people milling around. He brought an arm around her shoulders and Catarina closed the distance, fitting against his side as if she belonged there.

Sometimes she didn't act like the grieving widow he'd first expected. From the little Catarina had told him, her dead husband had not been a nice person, and even a less nicer husband. Could she be moving on? Did Afonso have any chance of winning her heart?

If he did, it was too soon to make any confessions. As well as this evening was going, she was likely to raise her walls if he did anything foolish and premature. His contract wouldn't be done until the last week of October. He still had some time.

"It's been two months since I arrived at Sunset Manor," he said as they watched the city lights turn brighter when the night grew darker.

Catarina leaned away to look up at him. "Two months?" She sighed. "It feels like we've known each other longer than that," she added after a pause.

"It does, doesn't it?"

"When's your last day?"

"In exactly thirteen weeks from today."

Two months had passed too quickly, and three would go almost as fast. But now that he had Catarina in his life, how could he even think of moving on without her?

A breeze ruffled the trees in the courtyard, and Catarina tightened her hold around his back. Afonso reciprocated, pressing his arm around her shoulder.

"What are you going to do when you leave?"

Her tone was uncertain as if she feared his reply.

It was his turn to let out a sigh. "I don't know yet." After a moment, he relaxed his hold on her and turned to see her better. "Catarina, I don't mind changing whatever plans I make in the future. Not for something better. Or for someone. Do you know what I'm saying?"

She sucked in a breath. "I—I think I could be falling in love with you, Afonso. I'm sorry I can't say more. Can you be patient with me, please?"

He nodded, keeping the eye contact with her. He could wait. If there was one thing he'd learned in jail was how to be patient.

When her hands splayed on his chest, Afonso brought his to her face. He brushed a kiss on her lips and she opened her mouth to him.

Maybe she was beginning to fall in love, but he was already there, and the words he wanted to say could wait until she was ready to hear them.

For now, Afonso poured all his feelings into that one kiss.

CHAPTER THIRTEEN

$\mathcal{I}$n the days following his dinner with Catarina in
Castelo Branco, Afonso couldn't stand being far apart
from her. He found tasks that kept him around the
house, and he even came in for lunch every day, but
eventually he returned to his large projects around
the property.

Catarina had her own work, finishing the sketches
of the manor and planning the rest of the decorating. They still had their evenings together, first by
the swing, then in the music room with him playing
and her listening. On the weekend, she continued
her quest for accent and art pieces now that the large
furniture for the ground floor had all been purchased.

Sometimes, when he walked her to her bedroom
door at the end of the day, Catarina would go on her
tiptoes to brush a kiss on his cheek. She'd flatten her
hands on his chest, not giving him a chance to bring
her closer to him.

The way he felt about her, maybe it was a good thing.

For now.

Today, Afonso had worked on the perimeter by the southwest wall that ran along the country road. No shade all day.

One more week until the middle of the month. August had started out as hot as the end of July, but the extended forecast promised cooler temperatures and some rain. The respite would be welcome.

On the way back from the east field, Afonso saw the Silvas returning to the caretaker house. He slowed down the ATV and held a hand up to return their greeting.

After a quick shower, he went looking for Catarina. He'd packed a lunch to save time coming to the house, but he'd missed seeing her.

As he made his way through the manor house, a scream rent the air from the outside. Afonso stilled, and his body went cold, hairs raised at the back of his neck. He ran to the front door and yanked it open. Past the rose garden, by the largest linden tree, Catarina was on her hands and knees on the grassy knoll by the swing.

"Catarina!"

She tried to get up and fell.

When Afonso got to her, she lifted her head. She was crying, and breathing hard and he went down on his knees next to her.

"What happened? Are you hurt?"

Her hair tumbled forward, covering her face, and he held it back.

"The swing broke," she said between pants.

"What?" Afonso lifted his head to the swing. Sure enough, the rope on the right side was broken, and the seat hung down, unsupported.

"I was sitting on it—then it broke from under me."

Afonso supported her arms and slowly lifted her from the ground until she sat with her legs spread out in front of her, covered by the length of a dress with a torn hem. Her hands were scraped with red scratches, and she placed them, palms up, on her lap, wincing.

"I'm sorry—" She hiccuped on a sob. "I'm sorry I broke the swing."

Afonso rubbed her back gently. "I don't care about the swing. I can fix it later." He scooted forward and took the broken rope in his hand.

But it wasn't broken—it had been cut through three-fourths of the way.

Someone had cut it on purpose.

Blind hot rage coursed through him, and his eyes clouded.

Anabela. She must have done it.

Catarina grimaced and sucked in a breath. "I need to go to the hospital."

He returned to her side. "What's wrong? What do you need?" How much pain was she in?

"Go get the truck and take me to the hospital." She inhaled twice, and her face scrunched up in pain. "Please."

Instead of going around the house to the backyard, Afonso cut to the main door and ran indoors until he emerged on the other side. Luckily, the garage door was up. He jumped in the truck and brought it to the north, parking as close to Catarina as he dared, not caring about the trampled grass. He lifted her in his arms and placed her in the front seat.

As he came around and sat behind the wheel, he remembered he'd yet to buckle Catarina, but she'd done it already. "You should have waited for my help. Your hands must be killing you."

She shook her head but didn't reply.

He lifted the brake and shifted into gear. How fast could he safely drive? He flipped on the emergency lights.

Catarina hunched forward, eyes closed, cradling her belly.

His worry increased. How had she fallen? And where was she hurt? She looked to be more in pain than a simple fall warranted. He reached his hand over and squeezed her forearm.

Catarina remained silent, her eyes shut tightly, her cheeks stained with tears.

When her hands went around her middle more tightly, the dress stretched to the sides, revealing an unequivocal rounded belly.

She was pregnant.

The truck swerved for a moment as if to echo his shock. Afonso gripped the wheel and glanced at the road, then back to Catarina once more, uncertain

166

he'd really seen what he thought he had.

She clutched her middle, definitely rounded, but not nearly enough to be anywhere close to full-term. It must have—she must have conceived just before her husband died.

Afonso pushed the disturbing thought from his mind.

He was an idiot.

The signs had all been there, from the very first moment they met: the throwing up, the nausea, her lack of appetite, the dehydration that had warranted a hospital stay, all the times she'd passed on drinking alcohol, the way she'd been gaining a little weight in the past few weeks, and especially the times she pulled away from him and didn't let him get too close. Not like after their first kiss in the upstairs hallway.

Hugging her close would have exposed her secret. How could he have been so blind to it?

"You're pregnant," he said slowly. His hands tightened on the wheel again.

Catarina was crying now, her upper body trembling in silent sobs. He reached in the glove compartment and pulled out a wad of napkins. She took it and hid behind the scrunched paper, nodding.

"That's why you've been going to Castelo Branco once a month."

Another nod followed by a hiccup. "I wanted to tell you." Fresh tears spilled from her eyes.

"We can talk about this later," he said quickly. "Let's just get you to the hospital."

167

How he didn't get pulled over for speeding, he didn't know. And he didn't know what to say to her. Was there anything that would have made a difference?

Afonso parked askew, partially blocking the emergency entrance. He exited the truck, came around to the passenger side, and carried Catarina in his arms. She clung to him and buried her face in his chest, and the trusting gesture twisted his heart. He didn't have the time to think about what it meant.

When the automatic doors parted, Afonso went straight to the admissions door. "We need help!"

A male nurse pulled a gurney closer to them. "What happened?"

Afonso lay Catarina on it. "She's pregnant and she fell on her belly."

A female nurse came over and leaned toward Catarina. "What's your name, honey?"

Afonso followed them as they pushed the gurney to the row of sick bays. "Her name is Catarina."

"Can you talk, Catarina?" The nurse tugged on the stethoscope around her neck.

"Yes," Catarina replied feebly.

"Who's your doctor, Catarina?"

"Dr. Paula," Catarina replied in the same tone.

An older nurse with a clipboard approached Afonso. "How many weeks gestation?"

He shook his head. "I have no idea."

"Are you the husband?"

"We're not married."

"Almost seven months," Catarina said slowly, not meeting his eyes.

The doctor entered the sick bay, and the nurse pulled on the curtains until she stopped in front of Afonso. "Are you in or out?"

"I need to call her family."

She closed the curtains the rest of the way and gestured toward the waiting room. "Don't go too far. We still have questions for you."

Questions he didn't know how to answer.

"Sir, is that truck yours?" The admissions secretary came from around her desk and gestured out the main doors.

He'd forgotten about the truck. "I'll move it right now."

The keys still dangled from the ignition, and he blew out a breath of relief. That was the last thing he needed, someone to steal the truck and leave them stranded in Castelo Branco.

Afonso drove to the farthest corner of the parking lot and parked under a tree. He swung the door open and drew his phone out of his pocket.

Catarina was pregnant, and it was about time her family knew, whether she liked it or not.

Catarina woke with a start and clutched the blankets. The room was semi-dark, and her eyes took a moment to adjust. She was at the hospital.

The memory came to her. She'd fallen off the swing and Afonso had found her on the ground. By the time they arrived at the district hospital, she'd been hysterical. They must have given her something to calm down. When she moved her arms, the weight of a blood pressure cuff around her left upper arm tugged back, and an IV was connected to the other arm. A wide band with a fetal monitor wound around her middle, and the dry staccato of her baby's heartbeat sounded softly from the machine nearby.

She let out a long sigh and relaxed immediately. The baby was okay.

Her hands and knees had been tended to, bound in dressings and medical tape. Someone must have helped her into a gown, but she had only a vague memory of a nurse talking gently to her.

"How are you feeling?" Afonso sat on a chair partially hidden by the curtain.

When she turned to him, he scooted the chair closer to the headboard.

"You're here," she said, her voice strangely breathless.

"Of course I'm here." He reached for her hand and squeezed her fingers. "You had me worried for a while."

She grimaced. "I kind of freaked out, didn't I?"

"Maybe a little, but it's understandable." He tipped his chin toward the monitor. "The little guy seems to be doing okay."

"Little guy?" She frowned. Did Afonso know something she didn't?

"Or little girl, I guess. Don't you know the gender of the baby?"

She shook her head. "I don't want to know. It'll be a surprise." She wouldn't be able to decorate a nursery, so knowing the gender hadn't been a priority. Besides, without someone with whom to share the news, what was the point? "Did I miss the doctor?"

"She said to come get her when you woke up." He let go of her hand and stood, but Catarina grabbed his arm.

"Afonso, please wait." He sat down but didn't take her hand. "I didn't think you were going to stay."

"You keep saying that. Did I give the impression that I was leaving?"

He was wonderful, always so patient and wonderful. "I've been keeping so many things from you and this one—"she lay a hand on her belly—"is pretty big. I'm sorry I didn't—"

The door opened, and a young doctor came in. "You're awake." A nurse with a portable sonogram machine followed the doctor. "And you look like you're feeling better."

"I'm a lot calmer."

"Your anxiety was a little high when you came in, so we gave you something to calm you down, and you fell asleep." She pushed the machine closer to the bed. "I know you were worried about the baby, so how about we take a peek?"

171

Catarina's heart jumped in her chest. "Right now?"

The doctor pressed the pedal to lower the front of the bed. "We can go if you don't want the ultrasound."

"I do," Catarina replied immediately.

Afonso stood. "I should go. I'll come—"

"No need to be nervous, Dad. You can stay and see your baby."

Afonso shook his head. "Oh, I'm not—"

Catarina grabbed his hand and squeezed tight. She wanted him to stay. She didn't want the doctor to think she was alone.

Afonso looked at Catarina, and she pressed harder, willing him to understand with a look what she couldn't voice aloud.

He squeezed back. "I'm not nervous." He dragged the chair to the head of the bed with his free hand and settled close to Catarina, holding her other hand.

The young doctor smiled and turned on the machine. "That's the spirit."

The nurse placed a folded sheet over Catarina's belly and then pulled up the gown until her skin was exposed. Catarina glanced at Afonso, who kept his eyes on the screen. If he was uncomfortable, he didn't show signs of it.

"Such a small belly you have," the doctor said. "Did you say you're seven months?"

"Not quite yet," Catarina replied. "I'll be twenty-seven weeks tomorrow. Dr. Paula says I've been consistently measuring small."

As the doctor slid the small wand on Catarina's belly, the images showed up on the screen, lighter and darker parts forming pictures of her unborn baby.

"That's your baby's head." The doctor moved the wand to a different position. "And there's the profile. Look at that little nose."

Tears welled up in Catarina's eyes. It had been a while since the last ultrasound, and the baby had grown noticeably.

"That's your nose," Afonso said, a smile softening his features.

Catarina laughed. He was right. The baby had her nose.

The doctor passed the wand, explaining what they saw as she showed the baby on the screen. Catarina marveled at the clarity of what she saw: her unborn baby moving, flexing the little fingers, opening his or her mouth. The emotion swelled in her heart at how much she loved the baby already.

"Do you know the gender of the baby?" The doctor moved the wand.

"No," she replied.

"Do you want to know?" The doctor asked.

"No," Catarina and Afonso said at the same time. His answer surprised her and she looked over at him. He shrugged.

The nurse smiled. "Good. You two agree."

"It's always awkward when the parents don't agree and one of them wants to know the gender and the other doesn't," the doctor said.

173

Afonso winked at Catarina, a playful smile tugging the corners of his mouth. "We agree."

He was covering for her, playing the game with such natural ease. She almost convinced herself she wasn't alone in this. Her heart squeezed, as if welcoming the lie.

A few minutes later, the doctor hit a button, and the machine printed a long strip of paper. "There you go, your baby's pictures." She stood and handed the long piece to Afonso. "Everything looks great with your baby, guys. No need to worry." She patted Catarina's foot under the covers. "Rest up, Catarina. We'll come check on you later."

The nurse pushed the machine out of the room, and the doctor followed.

Afonso sat there, holding her fingers in one hand, the other hand holding the sonogram prints. She couldn't gauge his mood. Was he mad at her for asking him to pretend to be the father?

"That was..." he finally said.

"I'm sorry. I shouldn't have asked you—"

"That was incredible, Catarina." He brought her hand to his lips and kissed her knuckles. "You are incredible, you know that?"

She inhaled quickly, surprise mingled with relief. "You're not mad?"

"Should I be worried you always expect the worst reactions from me?" He rose from the chair and bent to brush a kiss on her forehead. When he straightened, the wistful expression in his eyes made her breath hitch for a moment. "I'm not mad," he said softly.

Relief flooded through her, and she swallowed.

"Did he know?" Afonso asked. "Did Juan-Carlos know about the baby?"

Catarina shook her head. "I found out after he died." The words tumbled from her. "We were married for almost seven years, and he never wanted a baby. At first, I was too young and in love and I didn't mind waiting. But, as the years went by, this longing grew here." Her hands touched the spot over her heart. "I couldn't understand why he didn't want any children."

Afonso sat back down and reached for her hand again. He didn't interrupt or ask anything, just held her gaze and her fingers, and Catarina took courage to go on. "He was older than me by ten years, and his family wanted a grandchild so badly. But he let them think the problem was with me, and he never told me why. It even got to the point where he avoided me. Only occasionally, like that night last February when he was drunk and forced—" She stopped, feeling the heat on her cheeks and the tears in her eyes. Catarina wiped them with the edge of the sheet. "I was shocked when I found out I was pregnant. I didn't know what to think, or to do."

Catarina leaned back against the pillow and closed her eyes. What had she done, spilling her guts to Afonso like this? "I'm sorry. I shouldn't have dumped my problems on you." What he must think of her. At least now he knew, and she wouldn't blame him if he wanted to leave. "And I'm really sorry I didn't tell you I was pregnant. I—"

Afonso tugged on her hand. "There's nothing you need to apologize for." His eyes were gentle. "I'm not angry you didn't tell me, and I'm not going to quit being your friend, or anything like that."

How did he always know what she was thinking? Afonso understood her better in two and a half months than Juan-Carlos had in seven years.

"It will just take me some time to get used to the idea. You heard the doctor: rest up." He stood again, letting go of her hand, and she immediately felt the loss.

Of course he needed time. How could he not?

Catarina finally found the words as he reached to part the curtain. "Afonso, obrigada."

"Let's hope you still feel the same way tomorrow," he said, shrugging.

"Why? What's going on tomorrow?"

"I called your family. Your cousins should be here in the morning."

Dealing with Afonso was one thing. But her family was a completely different matter.

It was out of her hands and the realization came with a surprising sense of calm. She didn't have to decide whether or not to call her family.

Whether she was ready to face them or not, that was another question.

CHAPTER FOURTEEN

Catarina was finishing up breakfast when Afonso came in. The night before she'd been moved to an upstairs room in the women's ward for overnight monitoring, and the doctor had yet to come by this morning. For the time being, she was the only patient in the room.

Afonso poked his head through the curtains, and Catarina waved him in.

"How are you feeling this morning?" He pulled up a chair and sat near the bed.

"Much better, thank you." He didn't take her hand like he had the day before, and she missed it.

"How long do you have to stay?"

"Dr. Paula will be coming by during rounds, but I should be able to come home today." She touched her belly. "I have some bruising, but it was mainly anxiety. The baby is fine. I just overreacted."

"Given the situation, I don't think you did." He took her hand in his. "I'm glad you're both okay."

He pulled the sonogram print outs from this pocket. "I still have these."

"Can you keep them for me until I get home?"

He nodded and put them back.

"I'm sorry I led the nurse and doctor to believe you're the baby's father." The need to apologize wouldn't leave. "I know I shouldn't have done it, but I guess—I didn't want them to think I was alone."

"You're not alone, Catarina." He gave her fingers a squeeze. "I hope you know that."

Maybe not now, but soon it would be only her and the baby.

His phone buzzed, and he got it out of his pocket. He swiped at the screen and smiled. "I'm going now. Your other visitor is here." He stood and put the chair back against the wall.

"Who's here?"

"Your cousin."

"Which one?" There were quite a few on the Romano side alone.

"I'll see you at home." He smiled again and disappeared behind the curtain.

A few moments later, the door creaked open, and steps sounded on the floor. The curtain was pulled across, and it blocked Catarina's view to the door.

A woman's face poked around the curtain. "Is this Catarina Romano's room?"

Catarina's eyes widened. "Luciana! What are you doing here?"

Luciana sat on the edge of the bed, and leaned over to hug Catarina. They embraced for a long moment as the tears escaped her eyes.

"Prima," Luciana said. "It's so good to see you." She wiped at her own eyes.

Catarina could only nod as the emotion clogged her throat. It had been so long.

Luciana let go and dragged a chair closer to the bed. "I got a call from Filipe saying you might need a visit."

"Did anyone else come?"

"Only Filipe and Matias, but they said they had to talk to the groundskeeper about something. Not sure what that is." She frowned.

Catarina's shoulders dropped. She'd have liked to see her family.

Luciana reached for her hand. "Filipe and I talked about it, and we decided to wait before we told the others. We wanted to find out what you want to do."

Catarina nodded. Maybe that was best.

"That said, I think you should call your mom." Luciana reached in her pocket and handed a piece of paper to Catarina. "That's her phone number. I have to warn you that she won't be able to come right away. She broke a leg last month, and the doctor has restricted her travel."

Catarina twisted the edge of the sheet between her fingers. "Is she okay?"

Luciana smiled. "You know your mom. There's not much that will stop her. But your dad is being firm this time that she needs to listen to the doctor. So maybe you can call her after I leave." Her eyes misted. "I know how much she misses you."

Catarina swiped her cheek and nodded. She missed her mom so much. "I'll call her."

After a moment, Luciana's eyes lit up, and she grinned. "I can't believe you're pregnant. You're the first one of us to have a baby."

"Really? I thought Gabriela would have had one by now." Gabriela was the oldest girl cousin and had been engaged when Catarina left to Spain.

"No, that didn't work out for Gabriela. She's committed to her career." Luciana reached for Catarina's hand. "We have so much to tell you." She emphasized her words, but her attention shifted quickly. "I want to see your baby bump. It looks like you're barely showing."

Catarina drew back the sheet and pulled the gown tightly. "My doctor says I'm measuring small, but it looks big enough to me."

"How far along are you?" Luciana asked.

"Twenty-seven weeks today." Catarina sighed. Only thirteen more weeks until she met her baby.

"You're definitely not big," Luciana said. "I had a client last month who was twenty-three weeks along, and she looked so much bigger than you. Is it a boy or a girl?"

"I don't know," Catarina replied "I want it to be a surprise." She shrugged apologetically.

"You don't want to know?" Luciana raised an eyebrow. "How did you decorate the nursery?"

"I don't have a nursery." Catarina didn't have anything for the baby. "All I have is a stuffed lion from Chicco that plays Brahms' lullaby." She wouldn't be telling her cousin that sometimes she slept with the toy, comforted by the melody and what it meant to her. It was the first baby item she'd bought, and she'd only added a few items of basic clothing since then—she must be the most unprepared expectant mother her cousin had heard of.

Luciana raised an eyebrow and smiled. "Now I understand what my brother meant when he called."

"What did Filipe say?"

"He said you might need me to go shopping for you."

Catarina's eyes widened. "Shopping for what? I don't know what I need." She'd been meaning to start a list, but she'd lacked the emotional courage to do it when so much of her life was insecure. Her meager savings hadn't helped either.

Luciana drew a tablet from her purse. "It's never too late to start a list. And we'll make a Pinterest board, just in case."

Somehow, with her cousin beside her, everything looked a little brighter for Catarina.

Afonso parked the truck by the back patio and took the shopping bags to the kitchen. With guests arriving today, he'd bought extra groceries to accommodate three other adults. He wasn't sure how long they'd be staying, and he'd rather have too much than not enough.

Filipe and Matias sat at the table when he entered. Afonso placed the bags on the counter and greeted them.

"Do you have more bags in the truck?" Filipe asked. When Afonso told him yes, Filipe left to get them.

Matias stood and shook Afonso's hand. "It's good to see you. Filipe showed me what you've been doing on the property. Impressive work."

"Thanks. I enjoy it a lot." He was even considering opening a small business in gardening and grounds maintenance.

Afonso carried the rest of the groceries to the pantry, then returned to the kitchen. "Did you guys figure out the sleeping arrangements?" They had enough space for everyone, but not enough beds.

Filipe stuffed all the plastic grocery bags in a drawer. "We brought enough air mattresses. I'm taking the room I had last time, the one across from you. Matias will be staying in the room next to the bathroom in the east wing."

Filipe walked to the fridge and passed beer bottles to the other men, then rinsed a small bowl of lupini beans and set it on the table.

"What about Luciana?" Afonso asked.

"She's bringing Catarina home sometime today, and she said she wants to stay in Catarina's bedroom," Filipe said. "There's enough room."

"I bet she's planning a slumber party," Matias said with a chuckle.

"We took a quick tour. The ground floor looks great." Filipe said. "I'd seen the pictures Catarina emailed me, but it looks much better in person. I hope she has time to do the upstairs floor as well, starting with the suite."

"Was the suite yours before Catarina came?" It hadn't occurred to Afonso before, but it only made sense.

"I wanted to give her the best room in the house." Filipe shrugged. "I didn't know what else to do for her. I'm just glad I was able to get her when I saw the news her husband had died."

"At least she let you help her," Matias said.

"So it's true she hadn't been in contact with the rest of her family." Afonso set the bottle down, not in the mood to finish his beer.

Matias nodded. "Not since she left to Spain after graduating from high school."

"I'm glad you brought her," Afonso said to Filipe. It could have turned out much worse for Catarina.

Filipe set his drink down, and his smile faded. "I gotta admit I was surprised when you told me she's pregnant. I thought her sickness was related to the shock of losing her husband and all the stress that followed."

"You wouldn't have known when you left. She was still too early to show. I've been living in the same house since then, and I didn't notice either." Afonso had been too focused on his feelings for her and had missed all the clues. "According to what the doctor said, she's measuring small."

"I wonder why she didn't tell anyone?" Filipe asked.

"Perhaps she needed time to come to grips with it," Afonso said.

Matias leaned forward. "How have things been between the two of you living in the same house?"

Afonso shrugged. "It's hard to tell. Especially now."

"But you have feelings for her, don't you?" Matias asked.

Feelings didn't begin to describe it. "If you're trying to find out if I like your cousin, I do. A lot. As for the rest, I have no clue."

"Do we ever have any clue?" Filipe said.

Matias chuckled, and Afonso joined him. How right Filipe was. Was any man ever sure of what to do about the woman in his life?

Filipe and Matias traded a pointed look. "Well, since her father and older brother are not here to ask the pertinent questions," Matias started, "we will. How do you feel about Catarina being pregnant?"

Filipe nodded.

Afonso passed a hand through his hair and blew out a breath. "Honestly, I feel like I got the rug pulled from under me. I never planned for any of this. I came here to work and try to put my life back together, and I wasn't planning on falling in love. But I love her." He paused to look at the men in front of him, men who were family to the woman he loved. He'd been wanting to say it out loud and it felt so right. "I love her and, if last night is any indication, I'm pretty sure I'll be able to love her baby as well."

"What happened last night?" Filipe asked.

"I had the chance to be there when Catarina had an ultrasound. It was—" Afonso paused to get his emotions under control. "It's a miracle, you know. But at the same time I never planned to take on parenthood anytime soon, especially when my life is still so messed up."

Matias cleared his throat. "Does she know you love her?"

Afonso dropped his head and shook it. "I've tried showing her, but I haven't told her." He looked up again. "But it hurt when I found out she's pregnant. I know it's illogical, but it almost feels like she cheated on me. She's carrying another man's child." It had made him crazy to think of her with another man, and to know the circumstances had not been entirely consensual made him feel like murdering a man who was already dead.

"I understand how you'd feel that way, but you know she was married to him," Matias said.

"I do know that, but it doesn't make it any better." Especially when he and Catarina had shared two amazing kisses that had led him to believe she was interested and available when it might not be entirely true.

Filipe straightened in his chair. "If you don't see a future with Catarina and her baby, then maybe it's better you walk away now."

"What if she can't see a future with me?" He still didn't have any prospects when this job was over. Why would Catarina want to be with him? Afonso let out a long breath.

"It sounds like the two of you have some issues to talk over," Matias added.

Afonso nodded. "Lots and lots to talk over."

"Okay. Moving on to the next problem," Filipe said. "Why did you say Catarina's fall was not an accident?"

Afonso stood. "Let's go in the library. I left the tablet there, and I have something to show you."

As they passed through the music room, Filipe pointed at the piano. "How bad does this piano sound?"

"The piano sounds great. Catarina had it tuned. She had a guy come all the way from Coimbra to do it as a surprise for me." The memory warmed Afonso's heart.

Filipe whistled. "That must have cost a small fortune. I'd say she likes you."

Afonso wanted to believe she more than liked him.

Once in the library, Afonso retrieved the tablet from the drawer, and the men sat on the leather sofa and chairs. Afonso brought the app up and scrolled through the files, then set the tablet in front of everyone.

"What happened yesterday?" Matias asked. "Was Anabela involved?"

"I'm pretty sure she was, but I can't prove it. With the accidents and mishaps around the property, plus the incident when Catarina and I were pushed off the road, I became suspicious that Anabela might be behind all this." He tapped on the screen again. "I bought several surveillance cameras and installed them around the outside of the house."

Matias and Filipe leaned closer as Afonso showed them the locations.

"Catarina thinks the rope on the swing snapped or broke, but I made that swing myself. The rope was top quality. I inspected it, and it was almost cut through." Afonso brought up several stills and showed them to Filipe and Matias. "It's not very clear from this angle, but you can see two figures wearing caps and sunglasses stopping by the swing early yesterday morning. I must have been on the other side of the property already."

"It could be anyone," Filipe said.

"That's true, but who else? It's like her MO, causing accidents and messing with people's heads.

Matias nodded. "It sounds like something she would do."

"Why has Anabela followed you here?" Filipe asked. "And how did she know your location?"

Afonso raised his shoulder. "No idea. She hasn't contacted me yet. She might have placed a tracker on my phone. She had access to it several times.

I had the phone returned to me when I was released, and I turned it back on. It would have been pretty simple to pick up my location."

"So what's the plan?" Filipe asked.

"I think we need to contact law enforcement in Sete Fontes and Castelo Branco," Afonso replied.

If Anabela came close again, they'd be ready for her.

CHAPTER FIFTEEN

When Catarina arrived at the house, Afonso was waiting for her by the garage. He smiled at her, and she grinned back like a child. It had barely been a whole day, and she'd missed him so much. His departure in late October would break her heart in little pieces. What was she going to do without Afonso in her life? She brushed the thought aside and focused on the man instead.

He came around the car and opened the door for her. "You're home."

Was that longing in his eyes? The intensity of his expression left Catarina breathless for a moment. Had he missed her too? They'd seen each other almost every day since he'd arrived at the house. Living in such close proximity had brought on a sort of intimacy she'd never expected when they met.

Before she had a chance to say no, Afonso lifted her in his arms. "What are you doing? I can walk."

"I'm sure you can," he said, "but you're not going to say no, are you?" He winked at her and her face heated. He pressed her closer, and Catarina tightened her arms around his neck, pushing aside the guilt for enjoying it too much.

Luciana ran ahead to open the door. "She certainly will not be saying no."

Afonso carried her all the way to her bedroom and set her gently on the bed. "The guys and I are going to Castelo Branco. Will you girls be okay?"

Luciana stood by the door, holding it open. "You don't have to worry. I'll take good care of her."

"I'm sure you will." He turned to Catarina. "Call me if you need anything."

After he left, Luciana sat at the foot of the bed. "There goes a guy who has eyes only for you."

Catarina sat back. "I'm needy enough to believe you and pretend it's true."

Luciana chuckled. "Of course it's true. Have you seen the way he looks at you? How long have you lived together?"

Catarina spurted. "We are not living together. We're just living in the same house." She widened her arms. "This mansion. Afonso works outside every day. That's what Filipe hired him for. To be the groundskeeper. And besides, he's in the east wing and I'm in the west."

"Does that mean he's the beauty and you're the beast?" Luciana laughed at her own joke.

Catarina crossed her legs. "That's how I feel sometimes." Who would ever learn to love her with the past she had and such an uncertain future?

Luciana leaned forward and rubbed Catarina's hand. "Of course you're not the beast. I'm sorry for my lame joke. Can I ask what's going on between you and Afonso?" Luciana pulled a pillow onto her lap. "How does he feel about you being pregnant? And about your husband?"

Catarina sat back and sighed. "He only found out yesterday that I'm pregnant We talked a little, but I haven't told him everything about Juan-Carlos." Catarina took a breath. "It's hard to talk about it. I should never have married Juan-Carlos."

"I'm sorry," said Luciana.

"To answer your question, I don't know what's going on between me and Afonso. We had a rocky start. I judged him too harshly in the beginning." She'd take back her behavior if she could. "He's so kind and patient with me."

"I saw it. He even carried you up the stairs." Luciana reached for a cheese slice. "He definitely seems to have feelings for you. Do you know if he's hung up on someone from his past?"

"I don't think so, but this Anabela woman has been hard for him to deal with." Catarina said.

"Is this the same Anabela that Matias mentioned?" Luciana asked.

"Yes. She was the cruise director and Afonso was the pianist on the ship Matias captains."

"Afonso was a pianist? I thought he does grounds keeping."

"That's what Filipe hired him to do here, but on the *Princess Catarina* he played the piano. He even played in professional circuits in other European countries."

Luciana reached for the tablet in her purse. "What's his last name?"

"Cortez. Afonso Cortez," Catarina replied. He had an uncommon name and it suited him.

"Wow, look at this. He's got his own website." Luciana sat next to Catarina.

Catarina leaned over the tablet, unable to hide her curiosity. It was all there—his full name, birth date, where he was born.

Luciana snorted. "His middle name is Henrique? What was his mother thinking?"

"Maybe she's a royalist," Catarina said.

"She must be, to name him after the first king of Portugal." Luciana clicked on a YouTube link, and they watched him perform in a concert hall.

Catarina had heard him play in the music room, on an eighty-year old piano that had only been tuned recently. Watching Afonso play on a Steinway accompanied by an orchestra was a completely different experience.

"He's amazing," Luciana said in a reverent tone. Catarina wasn't the only one in awe of his talent.

The page also included his academic achievements, awards, and the highlights of his musical career, with all the cities he'd played in.

"Why did he stop playing?" Luciana asked.

"I think it had something to do with him being in jail," Catarina said.

"It says here he played in Barcelona." Luciana pointed at text on the screen. "Didn't you live in Spain with your husband?"

"We split our time between Barcelona and Lisbon." Juan-Carlos had never been content in one place.

"Did you go to classical concerts?" Luciana glanced up at Catarina as she scrolled through more pages.

"We did sometimes." Mostly as an opportunity for Juan-Carlos to show off and be seen.

Luciana looked up. "You could have met Afonso then."

Catarina scooted against the headboard, backing away. "I guess that's a possibility, but I think I would have remembered."

Luciana typed on the screen. "What was your husband's name?"

"Juan-Carlos de Aragón y Vega."

Luciana kept busy for a few minutes. Then she gasped. "You gotta see this, Catarina."

Catarina leaned forward and took the tablet Luciana handed to her. Her eyes locked on the group picture on the screen: Afonso stood in the center, his hair slicked back, his face smooth, wearing a black tuxedo with tails, and a big smile on his face; to his right, the maestro of the symphony and the mayor of Barcelona; to Afonso's left, Juan-Carlos in his dark gray tuxedo and Catarina in a bright red ball gown. The caption read in Spanish: *Afonso Cortez, Portu-*

guese pianist of acclaimed fame, with Mayor Santiago Iriarte, maestro Jean-Claude Rémy, and patron of the arts Barcelonian Juan-Carlos de Aragón y Vega, with his charming wife Dulce.

"Is that you?" Luciana asked.

Catarina nodded.

"Why does it say Dulce?"

"That was the name he gave me when we met, and he wanted me to change it when we married, so I did."

"Wow, Catarina, I barely recognized you," said Luciana.

Catarina hardly recognized the young woman staring back at her, a subdued smile on her red lips. The blonde highlights in her hair covered her natural brown color, and her expertly applied makeup gave her the plastic-perfect look Juan-Carlos always preferred. It used to take her an hour to put that face on, the face she used to hide behind.

Juan-Carlos, as always, had the confident smile of a man who always got what he wanted.

"Oh my goodness," Catarina whispered, raising her fingers to cover her tremulous lips. "Afonso asked me if we'd met before."

"When did he ask you that?"

"The day after we met, here at the house. He said I looked familiar, and I thought he was giving me a bad pickup line." She blinked, willing away the tears clouding her eyes. "I don't even remember meeting Afonso. Juan-Carlos dragged me with him to everything he attended, always staging photo ops. I was only his arm candy."

Luciana gave her a side hug. "The picture has a date of four years ago."

Catarina wiped a tear. "That sounds about right. I'd found out he'd had another affair, and he'd come home with apologies and gifts, as he always did. Then we'd be on display for the next month, so everyone could see how well things were between us." She handed the tablet to Luciana and buried her face in a pillow with a groan. "My life was so messed up. *I* was so messed up that I met Afonso and I don't even remember."

"I'm sorry you went through so much with your husband. Why didn't you reach out to your family? Or to me or Filipe?" Luciana asked softly.

Catarina shook her head. "How could I? Do you remember how I practically ran away from home to go to Spain? I told my parents I didn't need anyone anymore. Tiago tried so hard to reason with me, and the twins just looked at me like I was a stranger." She'd dismissed her parents and her brothers, the oldest and the two younger ones alike. "By the time I realized the kind of man Juan-Carlos was, I couldn't face anyone, and I certainly didn't have the humility to ask for help."

Luciana handed her a tissue, and Catarina wiped her tears. "I'd barely finished high school, and he was so charismatic and experienced. I felt like I'd won the lottery when he asked me to marry him and we eloped to Mallorca. He lived a lavish life, and he brought me right into it. Apartment in Lisbon, family home in Barcelona, weekends in Mallorca and Saint-Tropez. Servants, chauffeurs, personal chefs. Anything you can think of, we had it. The first few months were a whirlwind." She could still remember the dizzying lifestyle. "The beginning of the problems started creeping up around our first anniversary and by the second one, I knew he had lovers." Catarina never knew how many there had been; that was something she'd never wanted to know. "Last year, I started suspecting he was in financial trouble, but he wouldn't say anything about it. On the night he died, the embezzlement was exposed in the media, and the police were on their way to apprehend him when he tried to get away. He lost control of his car and crashed."

"Oh, sweetie," Luciana said in a low voice. "How did you come to stay here?"

"Filipe ran in the same circles, and we'd see each other at parties some times. There was a big scandal after Juan-Carlos' death. Pictures of him and his lover at the woman's apartment that night, and of him fleeing the police. The paparazzi camped outside our home. Because of the embezzlement, all the assets were frozen, and I had nothing. When Filipe came for me, I got away with a suitcase full of clothes and some personal items." She sighed and cradled her belly. "And then I found out I was pregnant."

"What are you going to do, Catarina?" Luciana asked.

"I don't know." She shrugged. "All I know is I'm going to have this baby. That's the only sure thing I know."

"What about Afonso?"

"With all his mistakes, Afonso is a much better person than I am. You know what I did when he told me he'd been in prison?" Luciana shook her head. "I yelled at him." Definitely something she wasn't proud of.

Slowly, Catarina stretched her legs, rose from the bed, and made her way to the window. She gestured outside. "He made that swing for me."

Luciana rushed from the bed and stood beside Catarina. "He made it?"

"From scratch. From chestnut wood he found on the property."

"Is there anything he can't do?" Luciana went back to the small table where Dona Madalena had put down a tray of snacks earlier in the day. "Tell me he's not a good kisser, or I'll be really jealous."

Catarina sat against the headboard with a smile on her lips. "Sorry, prima, but he can kiss." Oh, how he kissed.

"Have you two had a chance to lay everything out?" Luciana asked.

Catarina shook her head. "I don't have the courage. He'll be done with the contract before my due date, so he might not be here when I have the baby."

"He won't do that," Luciana said.

"I guess I have two months to figure it out,." Catarina said, half-heartedly.

Until then, she had other relationships to mend. She picked up her phone. "I think it's time I talk to my mom."

Luciana's expression softened. "I'm here for you."

Afonso leaned against the linden tree. He'd replaced the rope on the swing, and it rocked gently in the evening breeze, the seat empty. Catarina wouldn't be coming for a few days. Going up and down the stairs took too much energy, and she needed the rest.

And he needed the time to think.

With the preoccupation that came with Catarina's accident and her cousins who arrived after it, Afonso had been focused on making sure everything went well. He'd purposefully pushed his reaction to Catarina's pregnancy to the back of his mind, not wanting to deal with it until he had some time alone. Here he was now, unable to cling to the excuse of busyness anymore.

The discovery had taken him by surprise. But he'd been honest with her—he wasn't angry that she was having a baby. Although he understood why she'd kept it a secret, he couldn't help the twinge of disappointment that she hadn't trusted him. How many other secrets was she keeping from him? Keeping secrets never led to anything good, and he didn't want to make the same mistakes. Was he ready to share his heart with someone who didn't open hers to him?

Afonso reached for a leaf on a low branch. Soon the leaves would lose their green. The long days of summer were nearly gone, and the nip in the air foreshadowed the upcoming change of seasons. Even the sunset was shorter today, as if in a hurry to let the night come earlier. Already Afonso missed all the evenings he and Catarina had spent under this tree, talking and watching the colors linger in long stretches over the village of Sete Fontes.

Matias and Filipe had left on Sunday after breakfast. Luciana had stayed Monday and Tuesday and had returned to Lisbon today after breakfast, with lots of promises of a quick return.

The manor sounded empty with all of them gone. It was back to Afonso and Catarina with the Silvas during the week. Just like before, yet nothing was the same anymore.

He'd come to Sunset Manor thinking he'd be safe to rebuild his new life, and his past mistakes had followed him here. Even with the security cameras recording from strategic locations, and the daily patrols he and Senhor Francisco did, safety was elusive and no more than wishful thinking. How was he going to protect Catarina and her baby? Anabela was unstable. Whatever drove her actions was beyond the common sense and reason of a normal person. Who could even begin to guess what else she had planned?

The frustration mounted inside him. If only there was more he could do to anticipate Anabela's next move. As the sun dipped behind the far valleys, Afonso walked to the front door and entered the manor, then turned the lock and set the alarm.

A chink of light peeked from under the door to the music room. When he opened the door, he found the new floor lamp set to the lowest brightness. Catarina had bought it the week before, and he liked how it added to the sense of coziness by the upholstered chairs. Afonso crossed the room to switch if off.

"Boa noite," a voice said from the chair.

Afonso startled. "Catarina, what are you doing here?" The back of the upholstered chair had hidden her from his view.

"It's too early to sleep, and I'm really bored of resting. The silence upstairs is getting to me." She had her legs up and crisscrossed on the seat, and two large pillows behind her back, one on each corner. With the roundness of her belly in the way, he marveled she could sit comfortably in that position. Now that he knew she was pregnant, it was almost absurd that he'd never noticed it before. She wore the pink kimono, and the corner of his mouth rose in a closed smile.

Afonso took the other chair. "It's too quiet with your cousins all gone, isn't it?"

She let out a long sigh and nodded. "I kind of miss them." Her eyes rose to him. "Thank you for calling them."

"So you're not mad I did?" He'd worried about her reaction, but he'd wanted her to have the support of her family in such a time of need.

Catarina shook her head. "I'd forgotten how much fun Luciana and I used to have together."

His own childhood summers had been full of fun with cousins. He didn't have half as many as Catarina did, but he wished he could have the simplicity of those days. Like her, he'd lost contact with his extended family in the past few years, and he hadn't seen his parents and siblings since last summer. Maybe it was time he reached out.

She bit her lip. "I called my mom when I got home from the hospital."

Afonso leaned forward. "How did it go?"

"It was hard at first. I was afraid of her reaction. But she was just so happy to talk to me. We talked for two hours." Her lips rose in a smile. "We cried a lot, laughed a lot too. She wanted to come see me, but she broke a leg last month and doesn't have the clear to travel yet. Then on Sunday Luciana set up a Skype call with my dad and brothers."

"How many brothers do you have?"

"Tiago is the oldest. He's Filipe's age. The twins, Daniel and André, are five years younger than me."

"I'm glad you talked to them." Would Afonso ever get the chance to meet her parents and brothers?

She nodded. "Luciana and Mãe said they're throwing me a baby shower next month, and they'll bring the rest of the cousins and my Avó Teresa."

That answered his question. He'd be meeting her mother and grandmother, and more cousins. "That sounds like a lot of fun." Her unmasked joy lightened her expression as she talked about her family, and Afonso wanted to take her in his arms and kiss her. He leaned back in his chair and pushed the feeling away.

Catarina watched him curiously. Was she able to see through his feelings? He stood and put some distance between them. "Can I get you anything before we go to bed?"

Her eyebrow raised, and his neck heated at the blunder. "I mean, you go to bed in your bedroom and I go to bed in mine. I didn't mean *we* go to bed. Each bed. Separately." The more he tried to fix it, the worse it sounded.

Catarina chuckled.

"Will you let me know if you need anything?"

She straightened her legs and shuffled in her seat. "Yes. There's something I'd like you to do." Her hand rubbed her belly in slow motion. "Will you play something, please?"

Afonso made his way to the piano bench and sat down. "Any requests?"

She wiggled in the chair and rearranged the pillows as she got comfortable. "Maybe something soft and airy to calm her down."

"Her? Did you find out it's a girl?"

"I guess I'm hoping for a girl," she said with a small shrug.

Afonso touched his fingers to the keys with the first soft movements of a Chopin sonata. "A bedtime lullaby," he said over the music. The whispering of the melody crescendoed timidly, full yet delicate, and when the first sonata was done, he transitioned seamlessly to a ballad.

Catarina closed her eyes and leaned back. An expression of contentment took over her features, and her right hand came to rest on top of her belly.

He kept playing, warmth and contentment spreading through his body as he watched Catarina so relaxed. He wanted more moments like this, moments spent together at the end of the day.

After a few minutes, when she started nodding over her shoulder, Afonso wrapped up the last few notes and stood to nudge her. "Let's get you upstairs, mamã."

Her eyes opened, heavy with sleep, and she stretched, yawning. "I guess I am the mommy, aren't I?"

"Yes, you are." With a steady grip, he supported her up the stairs and down the hallway to the west wing.

When they arrived at her suite, Afonso switched on the light.

Catarina watched him for a moment, then stepped closer and kissed him on the cheek. As he walked to his bedroom, he took a breath.

It didn't feel right to be apart from her.

CHAPTER SIXTEEN

*O*n the morning of the baby shower, Catarina awoke to a knock on the door. Dona Madalena followed with a tray in her hands. "Bom dia. I figured you'd want an early start today."

Dona Madalena set the tray on the empty chair next to the bed, then lent a hand to Catarina to help her up.

The baby shower was today. Catarina smiled on her way to the bathroom, and she was still smiling when she walked back to the edge of the bed, where she sat down.

"Thanks for getting me up. I was so excited about the baby shower that I had a hard time falling asleep." She spread the fig jam on her toast and took a sip of the honeyed milk. The warm beverage tasted good. The days had shortened gradually in the past weeks, and the temperature had already dropped from the hot days of summer to the cooler ones of mid-September. She had also added a thin blanket to her bed. Even with the central heating in the house, she'd found that extra blankets, throws, and rugs throughout the rooms added a touch of coziness and comfort that was much needed.

Dona Madalena stood at the west window, cracking it open, as she always insisted on letting in fresh air in the morning.

Catarina took a large bite of the breakfast quiche, and Dona Madalena chuckled. "It's good to see you still have your appetite."

Maybe too much appetite. Catarina had moved her thirty-two week appointment to two days earlier in the week, from Friday to Wednesday, on account of the baby shower. Dr. Paula had measured her belly and declared it to be in the same small range as before, but to Catarina her belly had visibly grown larger this week. The baby complained of the tighter quarters as well, stretching and kicking and pushing around for space that was only growing smaller. Eight more weeks.

Dona Madalena and Catarina worked through the morning finalizing the last touches in the guest bedrooms. Afonso and Senhor Francisco had set up the new beds earlier in the week, and Dona Madalena had placed freshly washed sheets on each one. Afonso would be staying with Matias and the other guys in Castelo Branco, offering the use of his bedroom. As of last night, Luciana still didn't have an exact count on the number of family members coming to Sunset

Manor, and the thought made Catarina nervous. Thankfully, the pantry and fridge had been stocked to capacity, and lack of food would not be an issue.

She and Afonso had kept to their after-dinner tradition and spent some time outside at sunset. A much shorter time, now the evenings were colder. Once inside, Afonso had played the piano, and she'd watched him from the upholstered chair. The thought had occurred to her that even if given the chance to hear him play every day, it was unlikely she would ever tire of it.

Catarina and Dona Madalena talked about her family, and Catarina was grateful for the older woman's company while she waited for them to arrive. Excitement mingled with anxiety. They were coming to see her, to celebrate her baby's upcoming birth. After everything she'd done, and the lack of contact for the past seven years, Catarina didn't feel like she deserved the attention. Since Luciana's visit the month before, Mom had been calling her every few days, but they had yet to meet in person.

The sound of car horns interrupted her thoughts, and Catarina sat up. "They're here," she said to Dona Madalena with a nervous smile.

As Catarina rose from her chair, the back door opened wide, and Luciana entered, carrying bags in her hands. "We're here, querida." She dropped the bags on the floor and stepped forward to embrace Catarina. "Coragem, prima," she whispered in her ear.

Catarina nodded and pulled away from her cousin, taking in a deep breath. She needed courage, especially to face her mother.

Her cousin Jacinta and a blonde woman came in next, also carrying bags.

Catarina greeted her cousin. "Jacinta, it's so good to see you."

Jacinta kissed her cheeks, then stepped back and introduced the woman. "This is Vanessa Clark, soon to be Vanessa Romano. She's Matias' fiancée and practically one of us," she said in English.

Vanessa smiled and hung back. "I hope I'm not intruding."

Catarina turned to Luciana. "My English is terrible." Spanish was second nature to her, but English came harder. She'd had a few years of classes in high school but hadn't had the chance to practice in a long time.

Jacinta replied in English. "Vanessa has Portuguese family too, but she was raised in America. Her Portuguese is getting much better and she understands well enough."

Vanessa wiggled her hand. "Um pouquinho." She reverted to English. "I understand a bit, but speaking is harder."

After greeting Catarina, Jacinta and Vanessa walked to the pantry to leave the bags they carried.

Tia Celestina and cousin Gabriela greeted Catarina with kisses, hugs, and smiles as if they'd last seen her seven months ago, instead of seven years. The emotion welled in Catarina's heart, and when they stepped away, Mãe and Avó Teresa stood in front on her, already with tears in their eyes. Her own tears stained her face, and when they opened their arms, Catarina stepped forward and threw her arms around them both.

Words didn't come. She felt nothing but the love surrounding her.

After a moment, mom's hands rested on her cheeks, then on her belly. "My first grandchild."

"Is it a boy or a girl?" Avó Teresa asked.

"I don't know yet. I'm waiting until the birth." Catarina wiped her tears.

Avó Teresa placed a hand on Catarina's belly. "You can start buying blue. It's a boy."

"How can you be sure, Avó?"

Avó Teresa raised an eyebrow. "I'm only wrong fifty percent of the time."

Catarina laughed, and her family joined her.

"This is it," said Luciana. She looked around, including everyone. "Tia Glória wanted to come, but she couldn't get time away from the salon this weekend. Juliana is working too, and Susana and Anita are away at the university. As for the guys, only Matias and Knox came. They're staying in Castelo Branco tonight, and they'll come by tomorrow."

"Who's Knox?" Catarina asked.

Luciana gestured to Jacinta, who raised her hand. "He's my boyfriend." Her cheeks colored.

"You're stuck with us." Luciana grinned.

Catarina chuckled. "I'm glad I am. I just can't believe all of you came all this way for me."

The rest of the day went by too quickly amid food and laughter, stories and tears. These women were her family and her friends, and the bonds that linked them together went beyond years of separation and long nights of grief. Catarina took strength from them, from their presence and their hugs, and deep down she knew this was how she wanted her child to be raised, among women who'd love the baby as much as she did.

In the evening, after another round of cooking and eating, the Romano women moved to the music room for the baby shower. Afonso had temporarily moved the sofa and leather chairs from the library to add more seating options.

Luciana brought her gift first. "I've knit a lot of baby clothes, but this one is for an extra special baby." She placed a shallow box tied with a yellow satin ribbon on Catarina's lap.

"I didn't know you knit." Catarina tugged at the ribbon, then drew apart the layers of white tissue paper. Inside, nestled on clouds of more paper, the softest green knit romper was folded along with matching booties and a little cap with ear flaps. The delicate yarn and even stitches showed remarkable artistry.

"This is exquisite," she said at last, holding the little outfit in her hands. Catarina glanced at Luciana. "You knit this?"

Luciana nodded, a large smile on her face. "Do you like it?"

"I love it. It's so amazing."

"I'd like to knit your baby's christening set too, but I'll wait until the baby is born to see if I need pink or blue for the embellishments."

Catarina returned the ensemble to the box and passed it for the others to see. "Of course I'll let you."

Gabriela pushed a wrapped box in Catarina's direction. "After Luciana's amazing gift, none of the other gifts will compare, but here's mine."

"Gabriela, I've got nothing for this baby. You have no idea how much it means to me that you came from Porto to be here for the baby shower."

Her cousin blushed. "I'm glad I came."

The door squeaked, and Afonso's face peeked through the crack.

Luciana stood from her spot on the rug. "It's about time you got here."

Catarina couldn't have said it better.

Before Afonso had a chance to retreat, Luciana pulled him into the room. "Come on, I'll introduce you."

Afonso glanced at Catarina, his expression hesitant and almost timid.

Catarina winked at him.

Luciana turned to the room. "Everyone, this is Afonso Cortez, Filipe's groundskeeper. Among other things," she added with an eyebrow waggle toward Catarina.

Catarina ignored it.

Afonso took the introductions in stride, going around the room and greeting everyone with air kisses, charming them with his attractive smile, especially Mãe and Avó Teresa. When he got to Catarina, he brushed his cheeks against hers, and she flamed with a blush immediately. He'd shaved since she'd seen him last night, and the familiar scent of his aftershave filled her senses.

He reached for her fingers and gave them a squeeze, then straightened and faced her family again. "Ladies, it's been a pleasure, but I'll leave you to it."

"You're welcome to join us," Tia Celestina offered.

He took a step toward the door. "I still have to drive to Castelo Branco."

"We have tons of leftovers." Tia Celestina rose and took Afonso by the elbow. "Why don't you take some?"

"It's okay." He sent a pleading look toward Catarina. "I think we're going out."

Afonso kept edging toward the door, and Tia followed him.

Luciana stood and winked at Catarina. "Catarina is dying to know if you'll play something for us."

Oh no, she hadn't. Catarina waved him off. "Don't worry about it, Afonso."

His expression softened, and he smiled at Catarina. "How about I play something tomorrow?"

Catarina nodded back at him, smiling as well, and he waved at everyone.

After he left, with Tia Celestina right behind him, she found the rest of her family looking at her with knowing smiles.

"Look how cute you two are. You don't even need words between you," Avó Teresa said.

Mãe leaned forward in her chair. "How long have you two been living together?"

Catarina threw her hands in the air. "Not this again. We're not living *together*. Just living in the same house."

"And that's been how long?" Avó Teresa insisted.

"Since the end of May." Catarina said. Had it really been that long? Soon his contract would be over, and her baby would come after that. The emotion lodged in her throat.

"Almost four months." Avó said. "That's plenty of time."

"Plenty of time for what?" Gabriela asked.

Avó Teresa smiled and winked at Catarina. "To fall in love, of course."

Vanessa and Jacinta looked at each other and smiled. "More than enough time," said Jacinta.

Catarina knew that very well.

She'd had plenty of time to fall in love with Afonso.

Luciana reached for a small box and started passing white votive candles to each woman in the room. They sat in a loose circle around Catarina.

"In honor of the upcoming birth of the first Romano grandbaby, I propose a new tradition," Luciana said. She stood next to Catarina with a candle in her hand. "In the olden days, families lived much closer to one another. When the time came for a woman to give birth, her mother, grandmother, and sometimes older sister were in attendance. Other women in the family, such as aunts, cousins, and younger sisters wouldn't be. Because giving birth was always risky to the mother and the baby, the other womenfolk lit candles and prayed for a quick delivery and a healthy baby." She turned to Vanessa and spoke English. "In Portuguese, to give birth is *dar à luz*, which literally means to give to light, meaning the baby comes to light in the world." She went on in Portuguese. "When Catarina goes into labor, we'll send the word out to everyone and we'll each light our candle as a way to keep Catarina and her baby in our thoughts and prayers. Even if we can't come support Catarina in person, she will know we're thinking of her and she's not alone." Luciana smiled at Catarina.

Catarina wiped under her eyes. An overwhelming feeling of peace and love filled her heart, and she rested a hand over her chest. "That may be the most beautiful thing I've ever heard."

The sound of sniffling from around the room confirmed she wasn't the only one crying. Catarina stood to hug Luciana, and soon her mom, grandma, aunt, and cousins surrounded her as well.

This was the love of strong women. The love of her family.

Her family's departure weighed on Catarina, and she missed them dearly in the days following the baby shower. It didn't help that the weather turned rainy the next week, adding to her melancholy.

Unable to work outdoors, Afonso stuck to the house, rearranging furniture under her direction and helping her organize the baby gifts she'd received at the shower. He set up the bassinet and disposed of all the empty packaging, making a list she could later use to write the thank you cards. Catarina had him tuck the car seat and the baby swing into a corner of the suite, not knowing what else to do with the pieces. For all the sketches she'd drawn, she hesitated decorating a space for the nursery. How much longer would she stay at Sunset Manor after the baby's birth?

Afonso was patient and tender with her, assuming all the cooking and cleaning while the Silvas stayed in the village. He played the piano more often, and on the second night of being rained in, he set up a movie showing in the library, complete with popcorn and her favorite candy. Catarina moved aside the pillows he'd brought down and snuggled next to him. She ended up falling asleep on his chest, more content and at home than she had been in a long time.

The sun returned on Wednesday morning, and the Silvas followed a few hours later. Catarina hid a pout, wishing she and Afonso could have had more time alone. But reality had a way of opening her eyes to the naïveté of her dreams, and wishing for what she could not have only brought heartache.

On Thursday, Dona Madalena persuaded Catarina to walk to the swing after lunch. Afonso would be taking it down for winter soon and she wouldn't have many more chances.

When she returned inside to rest, he sat on the top step near the landing to the west side.

Catarina stopped short. "I thought you were working at the main gate today."

"We got the gate down and the new one will be here tomorrow." He stood and took her hand. "Can I walk you to your room?" A twinge of nervousness clouded his voice.

"Is everything all right?"

"All the times I went with you on furniture hunting trips rubbed off on me."

"Excuse me?" She arched an eyebrow at him.

He pushed open the door to her bedroom and gave her a lopsided smile. "Ordinarily, I wouldn't invite myself inside, but if you don't like it, I'll take it back down."

"Don't like what?"

Afonso gestured to the bassinet. Next to it, a midcentury dresser in a deep mahogany captured Catarina's attention.

They approached and Catarina stroked the gleaming wood. "This is beautiful, Afonso."

216

"I cleaned it and restored the finish, but it took longer to dry with the humidity this past week." He pulled a drawer in and out. "Do you think there's enough room for the baby's clothes?"

She nodded. "It's perfect." With three wide drawers on each side, she wouldn't be lacking space. "Thank you." She went on tiptoes and kissed him on the cheek.

Afonso dropped an arm around her back and brought her in for a side hug. "Now I'm trying to find a rocking chair before the baby's born."

Catarina rested a hand on his chest and closed her eyes, unable to form any words.

What would he say if she told him she loved him?

Catarina didn't sleep well. She thought about telling Afonso of her true feelings. All night she weighed the pros and cons, asking herself if she had the courage to do it. In the morning, she hadn't reached a decision.

When the Silvas left after lunch, Catarina walked to the library. Afonso and Matias had brought the boxes of books down from the attic the week before, and they'd filled the shelves on top. Catarina had been staging the lower shelves, having promised Afonso she wouldn't use the stepladder or lift boxes. She was glad to see the project nearly finished with only half a box worth of smaller volumes left.

Her phone pinged. Catarina drew it out from her pocket and swiped at the screen. It was Joana, the woman from the furniture warehouse.

Olá, Catarina. Are we still on for today?

Catarina suppressed a groan. With her family visiting for the baby shower last week, Catarina had rescheduled her appointment with with Dr. Paula for a different day.

Hi, Joana. I'm sorry. I won't be coming to Castelo Branco today.

That's okay. Is there another time that works better for you?

Catarina pulled up the calendar on the screen. With a few more weeks of work, she could finish the last of the decorating. Then the interior photos would look more professional.

I was actually thinking we could go ahead and schedule the photo op in the house. Would it work in a month from today?

Yes. That would be great. Let me check with my photographer what time he prefers, and I'll get back with you.

Perfect.

Catarina clicked on the screen and returned the phone to her pocket. Another project she was looking forward to. One that would bring money, for a change.

If only everything else was as easy.

CHAPTER SEVENTEEN

$\mathcal{T}$he laden skies had been swelling all day, threatening a downpour and somehow holding it in. Afonso took a breath, not finding any relief in the dense, heavy air charged with electricity.

The installation of the lightning rod and weather vane had been postponed for a clear day, and, with the impending storm, he'd sent the Silvas to their home in Sete Fontes a day earlier.

Catarina had mentioned someone was coming to photograph the furniture in the ground floor rooms, but Afonso hoped they'd reschedule for another day.

Before sunset, Afonso took the ATV and drove the perimeter of the property, checking for obstructions in the irrigation ditches. With a hoe in hand, he cleared the drainage, preparing for the rain that was sure to come.

His phone rang, and he stopped to remove his gloves. Seeing Catarina's number, he smiled.

"I should be home in twenty minutes," he said to her.

When she didn't reply, Afonso frowned. "Catarina?"

"Hi, Afonso. It's Anabela."

His stomach dropped. "What are you doing with Catarina's phone?"

"I wanted to make sure you answered."

A sour taste filled his mouth as he tried to think. "Is she okay? Let me talk to her."

"Catarina is fine. You and I have things to discuss. Meet me at the house."

He ground his teeth. "I'm coming."

"Afonso," she added. "No heroics. Do not call Matias or the authorities or anyone else. I'm armed and prepared to use it, if it comes to that."

Afonso disconnected the call and shoved the phone in his pocket. He threw the hoe on the ground then hopped on the ATV, revving up to the maximum speed.

Anger roiled inside him, heartbeat pounding inside his chest, his heart squeezing with a feeling so intense it stung. The fear for Catarina's safety—it brought a metallic taste in his mouth. How could he have been so distracted? He'd let his guard down, lulled by the false safety of Anabela's silence. She hadn't left; she'd merely been biding her time, planning her return when it was convenient for her.

He parked in the rear courtyard and jumped off the ATV, running to the kitchen door. A bearded man stood by the door, and Afonso stopped.

Afonso frowned. "Who are you?"

The guy smirked. "Doesn't matter. I'm here to make sure you don't do anything stupid." He put his palm out. "Your phone."

Afonso handed him the phone then made his way through the house with the guy on his heels.

In the entry hall, Catarina sat on a straight-backed chair in front of the dining room doors, her shoulders back and her posture rigid, a hand cradling her belly. Anabela stood nearby, halfway between the console and Catarina, a small handgun in her hand.

His heart jerked at the sight of the metal barrel. Anabela's behavior had escalated. She'd never used a gun on the *Princess Catarina*.

When Afonso took a step in Catarina's direction, Anabela held a hand up. "Not so fast."

Afonso stopped but turned to Catarina. "Are you okay?"

She nodded, and her lips pulled into a tight smile.

His fists balled at his side. "I'm here, Anabela." He kept his voice measured, trying to hide the tension coursing through him. "How did you get in the house?"

"What else do you want to know, Afonso? How I have Catarina's phone?" She raised her other hand and turned the screen to him.

"How did you do it?" He played her game, unwilling to take any risks until he knew what Anabela wanted. His first priority was to get Catarina away as soon as possible.

221

"I was the one who delivered the furniture back in July. Three months ago today, actually. Befriending Catarina was easy after that. But I started following you when you got out of prison." She shook her head slowly. "Tsk, tsk, tsk. That was not a smart move, Afonso. You shouldn't have ratted me out. It didn't do you any good, did it?"

Afonso half listened to Anabela's rants, focused on Catarina instead. She didn't look comfortable. She had a hand near her back, the other low on her belly. Was she in pain? Was it stress related or something else? Her doctor had said everything was going well at Catarina's thirty-six week appointment last Friday, and he clung to that hope. He had to get her to safety.

Afonso drew the keys to the Ford truck out of his pocket. "How about we go for a drive? You, me, and your henchman here." He tipped his chin in the man's direction. "We can leave Catarina behind. She's not involved in this."

Catarina frowned at his suggestion, and his heart twisted.

Anabela chuckled. "That's my younger brother, Nico. He's so much better than a henchman. More loyal too."

Afonso could see the resemblance now. The same eyes. The same wide forehead. The cold, calculated stare.

Anabela sighed and stood. "Okay, I'm getting bored with the small talk." She walked over to Catarina and rested her forearm on the back of the chair. Catarina leaned away to the other side.

Afonso clenched his jaw.

"Your girlfriend here has been lying to you," Anabela went on. "Her name is Dulce Vega, and she was married to Juan-Carlos de Aragón y Vega."

Catarina looked away.

Anabela laughed. "I'm guessing she didn't tell you that. People have been wondering what happened to Juan-Carlos' wife after he died. Imagine what they'll say when they find out she's been hiding in the backwoods of Castelo Branco. And she's pregnant too."

"This has nothing to do with Catarina. Tell me what you want from me, and I'll do it." Afonso kept his voice calm, even as the anger rose inside him.

Anabela moved to the side next to Catarina and rested a hand on her shoulder. Catarina flinched.

"I have video and photos of Catarina in Castelo Branco going to the doctor and shopping at baby stores, having dinner with you." Anabela raised an eyebrow. "How much do you think I can get for those? There are magazines that will pay top euro for exclusive content on Dulce Vega. I can do even better. Did you know the media is camped down in Castelo Branco for the next two days? Some sort of official visit with the prime minister. Election year." She shrugged. "You know how it is."

"No," Afonso said firmly. "You need to leave Catarina out of this. It's me you want, and I'll do whatever you ask."

"Afonso, no," Catarina interrupted him, her eyes wide.

"Just leave her out of this," he repeated to Anabela. "Whatever you want." He kept his gaze firm on her, trying to make her believe he was serious about his offer.

Anabela sneered. "I knew you'd step up. This is how it'll be—you have connections I don't, so I'm sending you to Porto with my brother. When you get there, you'll call Matias and ask him to get you aboard the *Princess Catarina*. Use whatever excuse you want; I don't care. I already checked, and the ship is not leaving on a trip until Sunday. I have a … parcel I need you to deliver to the lounge."

His stomach churned at Anabela's demands. "What sort of parcel?"

"One that will attract a lot of attention." Anabela smiled, self-satisfaction showing in her expression.

She was insane. Anabela had clearly turned crazy since last year. She was threatening Catarina practically at gunpoint, and now wanted him to deliver a bomb to the ship. He wouldn't do it, but he wouldn't let her know that. He just had to get Anabela away from Catarina. He'd deal with the rest when he got to Porto.

He took a breath and let it out quickly. "I'll do it."

"No!" Catarina rose in her seat, and Anabela pushed her back down.

"I'll go to Porto and do it, but you need to come with me."

"I'll come when I know you've delivered it. Until then, I'm staying here with Catarina. As an incentive for you to get the job done." She sneered. "Otherwise, I'll take her for a little drive, and who knows what might happen? The back roads in the interior of the country are not kept very well, are they?"

Afonso's shoulders dropped. He didn't have a choice. The only way to keep Catarina safe for now was to agree to Anabela's demands. Maybe if he tricked her into thinking he'd planted the bomb, she'd leave Catarina behind. Somehow, he'd have to neutralize Anabela's brother and call the authorities.

"I know you can get the job done," Anabela said. "Too bad you grew a conscience, or I could have finished this business months ago." She flicked her hand impatiently. "No matter. It'll be more symbolic this way. Tomorrow's the anniversary of our father's death. He worked for António Valadares." His expression turned hard. "And he died in the same accident that killed Vanessa Clark's mother. But they don't know that. None of them know that. They'll be thinking of Ana Catarina Valadares and what a sweet daughter she was, what a great mother and person." She spat the last word. "But not a thought spared to Manuel Avintes." She walked over to the console. "Tomorrow everyone will know who he was."

"Avintes?" The question slipped his mouth.

"I used my mother's maiden name so the company couldn't trace me back to my father."

She'd always been good with details, as he'd come to learn when he worked with her last year. Afonso swallowed. Of all the stupid mistakes in his life, falling for Anabela's charm had been the worst.

Anabela straightened her posture and held up the gun with confidence. "Let's go." She tapped Catarina's shoulder, and Catarina stood from the chair. "To the kitchen."

At the sight of the gun so close to Catarina, Afonso's body tensed. A bead of sweat ran down his back. He took a step in Catarina's direction, but Anabela's brother grabbed him by the arm.

Anabela took Catarina's elbow. "Walk on ahead, Afonso."

Afonso did as she said. Once in the kitchen, Anabela led Catarina to a chair at the table. "Where are the keys to the vehicles?"

Her brother pulled Afonso to the opposite side, away from Catarina.

"Which vehicles?" Afonso asked.

"All of them. The Audi, the Ford truck, even the four-wheeler."

Afonso drew the key chain out of his pocket and removed the keys. "That's for the truck and the ATV. I don't have the Audi's on me."

"Where is it?" Anabela asked in a sharp tone.

Afonso set the keys down on the tabletop. "In the library. First drawer on the right side of the desk."

Anabela jerked her chin, and her brother sprinted in that direction. She pulled up a chair and sat down, the gun pointing loosely in Catarina's direction.

His fingers twitched, and he flexed his hands. There was nothing Afonso could do. He wouldn't risk Catarina's life.

When Anabela's brother returned, he handed the Audi's key to his sister. Anabela gave him the key to the truck. "Go get it out of the garage." She slipped the other two keys in her pocket.

While her brother was gone, Anabela tucked the gun in the small of her back, then pulled out her phone and tapped on the screen.

Afonso turned his attention to Catarina again. Her expression was tight, and she still kept a hand on her side, the other hand rubbing slow circles on her stomach. She looked up at him, and her eyes softened.

This was his fault. It was all his fault. If he hadn't become involved with Anabela, none of this would have happened. But he had, and he couldn't change the past. He'd already paid for that mistake, and he was still paying for it. Coming to Sunset Manor was another mistake, and now Catarina was suffering for it.

"You two stop making googly eyes at each other," Anabela said, her glance hard and her voice dripping with irritation. "It's sickening."

The truck came to a stop just outside the back steps, and her brother jumped out. He entered the kitchen, a sheen of sweat rimming his forehead. How long had he been at his sister's bidding? Would Afonso get a chance to talk him out of delivering the bomb?

Anabela stood and gave him the gun. "You're going to need it." She turned to Afonso. "Don't get any bright ideas. Nico knows how to use it."

Her brother tipped his head in Catarina's direction. "Are you going to be okay?" He asked his sister.

Anabela chuckled. "Of course. What is she going to do? She's nine months pregnant." She touched his upper arm. "Just give me a call when you get to Porto."

Nico nodded then turned to Afonso and waved the gun at him. He threw the key at Afonso. "You heard Anabela. Don't get any ideas."

Afonso caught the key and hesitated. His eyes found Catarina's. So many things he wanted to say. Why hadn't he told her how much she meant to him?

She nodded at him, her gaze resolute.

When Anabela's brother jabbed him again, Afonso turned and exited the kitchen.

He could only hope he'd have a chance to tell Catarina how he truly felt.

As Afonso left toward the truck, Catarina rose from the chair and stopped at the glass door. She held up a hand and splayed it on the cool surface, resting her forehead next to it. Worry filled her chest.

Huge, black clouds hovered above them, and the sky rent with long-overdue rain. Afonso turned on the windshield wipers and blinked the lights twice in her direction.

"What do you think you're doing?" Anabela barked.

"I just want to see him leave." Catarina's voice strangled at the last word, and a tear rolled down her cheek.

Anabela laughed. "Go ahead. Watch him leave. It'll probably be the last time." She pulled out her phone and leaned back, head down toward the screen. "If he survives the blast or the showdown with the cops, he'll be put away for life. I can guarantee you that," she spat.

Catarina shuddered. She kept her eyes on the back of the truck as it disappeared around the house. Her breath fogged the glass, and she traced a shape on it.

It wasn't fair. How could this be happening to Afonso again? This psychopath woman was forcing him into crime in order to achieve her crazy plans of vengeance. Catarina had to stop this somehow. She wouldn't let Afonso go to jail for a crime he didn't commit. He didn't deserve it. He was too good a person, too good a man. He had done so much for her, always supporting her in everything, being the friend Catarina had desperately needed.

Avó Teresa was right—four months was more than enough time to fall in love, and Catarina loved Afonso with all her heart. Irrevocably. Why had she been waiting to tell him? She loved him too much, and she wouldn't let Anabela ruin his life again.

In a way, Anabela treated Afonso in the same manner Juan-Carlos had treated Catarina. Anabela was using Afonso, disregarding his needs, his safety, and even his basic rights. Catarina recognized Anabela for who she was—a manipulative person who didn't care about anyone else.

The first crack of lightening split over the courtyard, and Catarina flinched. The muscles in her belly tightened. She'd been having Braxton-Hicks contractions at irregular intervals throughout the day. Dr. Paula had told her not to worry about the false contractions, which could go on for weeks before she went into real labor. Maybe the stress had triggered them. She was tired, and her back hurt from the tension of sitting on the straight-backed chair in the entry hall.

Catarina returned to the nearest chair. An idea formed in her head. It was about time she took a stand to protect the man she loved.

"I need some painkillers," she said to Anabela. "My back is killing me." She stood and placed both hands over her kidneys, arching her back.

"You're not going anywhere." Anabela raised her eyes from her phone. "Sit back down and shut up."

Catarina perched on the chair, her hands on either side of her rounded belly. The baby had been active earlier but had calmed down after that. Exactly the opposite of Catarina's mood—she'd rested after lunch, saving her energy for Joana's arrival.

Only Joana hadn't come. Anabela had.

Catarina had completely fallen for Anabela's ruse. The thought filled her with a quiet anger, simmering low in her chest. Anabela was a masterful manipulator, a liar with no remorse and no scruples, using anyone in her path to accomplish what she wanted.

As her stomach tensed, Catarina leaned forward and moaned. She squeezed her eyes shut and let out little breaths until the pressure eased. Inhaling deeply, Catarina opened her eyes.

Anabela glared at her for a moment, then went back to her phone.

Catarina turned to Anabela. "So all the problems Afonso had around the property—you were behind all those."

Anabela smirked. "Not very much of a challenge. The fence is accessible in a lot of spots along the property."

"You cut the rope on the swing too," Catarina said.

"No, my brother did. And he only sliced it. He didn't completely cut it through." Anabela shrugged.

Catarina pursed her lips. "Do you have fun watching people get hurt?"

"It was a test to see if Matias came. And he did."

That fall off the swing could have been so much worse. Catarina turned away, her face hot with a simmering anger. Anabela was despicable, and she deserved to be put away for a long time. As soon as possible.

A few minutes later, another wave of tension seized the muscles in Catarina's lower belly. She shifted in her chair, trying to get comfortable, puffing out shallow breaths as a coping mechanism. She stood when it subsided.

"I told you to sit down," Anabela said, frowning.

"I'm not comfortable, and I really need to use the bathroom."

Anabela scowled. "You better not get any big ideas."

"Like you pointed out, I'm nine months pregnant. The only idea I have is to get some relief."

Anabela grabbed Catarina by the arm, and they walked to the service bathroom off the kitchen. Anabela inspected the interior, then waited outside the door until Catarina was done. On the way back to the kitchen, Catarina stopped and hung on to the wall, posture low and hunched forward, eyes scrunched until the wave of pressure passed.

When they arrived in the kitchen, Anabela propelled Catarina to the chair. Outside the French door, the storm held strong, wind and rain churning in a show of force. Hopefully it would abate soon. Thinking of Afonso driving in these conditions worried Catarina. But maybe the storm would delay Afonso's arrival in Porto, raising his chances of foiling Anabela's plan.

As soon as she sat down, Catarina cradled her belly. "I need to go to the hospital," she said through clenched teeth.

Anabela's expression hardened. "Whatever for?"

"I've been having regular contractions every five minutes." Catarina's mouth tightened in a flat line.

Anabela narrowed her eyes at Catarina. "Isn't that just great," she said in a monotone voice as she stood. "It's not my problem. I'm not taking you to the hospital."

Catarina's eyes widened. "Why not? The baby is coming whether I want it or not. Are you ready to help me deliver?"

Anabela made a face, visibly recoiling in disgust at the scenario. She frowned and paused for a minute, then pulled out her phone. "It's been an hour and a half since Nico left. They're well on their way to Porto, which means I can get going as well." She placed a hand on the handle to the sliding door. "I don't care what you do. It was Afonso I needed."

Catarina stood for a moment. "Can you at least give me the phone back?"

Anabela drew Catarina's phone from her pocket. "You mean this phone?" She opened the door and hurled it at the patio, where it landed on the granite steps in a heap of little pieces.

Catarina squinted through the rain as Anabela ran to the garage and entered through the lifted door. In the next minute, Anabela sped away in Filipe's Audi.

As soon as she was gone, Catarina straightened and walked to the cabinet drawer past the refrigerator. She grabbed a pen and a pad of paper and returned to the glass door.

She held her breath, hoping what she was about to do worked. Slowly, she formed an O with her lips and huffed on the glass. The truck's license plate appeared for a moment, and she copied it onto the paper. A small smile tugged at the corner of her mouth. It wasn't victory yet, but a start.

Walking as fast as she could, Catarina climbed the stairs to her bedroom. She'd been having contractions in the past hour, but not every five minutes. Just as Catarina had hoped, Anabela left when she believed Catarina to be in labor, unwilling to drive her or offer any assistance. Even the phone was gone.

Catarina looked around the bedroom. She spied the tablet under a pillow on top of the bed and retrieved it. Sitting on the edge of the mattress, she tapped on the screen, and hope flared inside her chest. Maybe her half-cooked plan would work after all.

She navigated to the contacts folder and found the Silvas' phone number, then called them. The Wi-Fi signal was strong, thanks to Filipe's zeal, enabling her to use the phone application.

When Dona Madalena answered, Catarina rushed to talk. "Dona Madalena, I need someone to give me a ride to Castelo Branco, please."

"What's going on?" Worry touched the lady's voice. "Is the baby coming? Is Senhor Afonso not there? Did something happen to him?"

"Can I explain on the way to Castelo Branco? I really need to get there as soon as possible."

"Of course we're coming. Hang in there, Menina Catarina."

They arrived in twenty minutes. Fortunately, the storm had abated by then, and she urged the couple to hurry.

By the time Catarina arrived in Castelo Branco, she was already tired. The Silvas wanted to drop her off at the hospital, but she needed to put her plan in motion if she had any hope of stopping Afonso before he arrived in Porto.

The city was busy as they drove through downtown. When they passed the five-star hotel, the sidewalk was crowded with photographers, and the parking lot full. Hadn't Anabela mentioned the media was in Castelo Branco for some political event? If the police didn't move fast enough, maybe Catarina would contact the gossip magazines. The whereabouts of Dulce Vega was still a hot topic, and it would draw attention. Catarina was desperate to stop Afonso and Anabela. Even if she had to talk to the paparazzi—she would do anything.

When Catarina arrived at the police station, she used the public phone in the waiting room to call Filipe. Dona Madalena dragged a chair, and Catarina sat down.

He answered with a smile in his voice. "Catarina, how are you? That baby coming soon?"

"Filipe, Anabela Rialto was at the house."

He sobered immediately. "How did that happen? Let me talk to Afonso."

"Afonso isn't here. She threatened me and made him drive to Porto to deliver something to the ship he used to work on." He tried to say something, and she interrupted. "I think it might be a bomb. There's no time. We need to send the police after their car and stop them. I'm at the police station in Castelo Branco. Didn't you and Afonso and Matias talk to a detective here?"

"We did. Ask for Detective Arantes and mention my name and Matias'." Filipe gave Catarina more instructions on what to say until he arrived. "I'll call Matias and tell him what's going on. Hey, are you okay? How did you get to Castelo Branco?"

Catarina let out a slow breath. "I called the Silvas, and they brought me here. Okay, I'll ask for Detective Arantes and give him the license plate numbers to the Ford truck and the Audi."

"I'll be there as soon as I can," Filipe promised.

Detective Arantes was on his day off, but at the mention of Sunset Manor and the Romanos, he arrived at the station within thirty minutes, willing to talk to Catarina.

By the time they were done, the weariness caught up with Catarina, and she allowed herself to relax in her seat. The false labor contractions hadn't let up, the flat annoyance of before verging on a dull, intermittent pain. She'd done all she could to stop Afonso from reaching the ship, to stop Anabela and her insane plans.

It was now out of her hands.

All she could do was trust and wait.

CHAPTER EIGHTEEN

$\mathcal{C}$atarina woke to the early sun spreading through the thin blinds, and she grabbed on to the sheet. The events of the previous night came to her.

Filipe had arrived in record-breaking time, and he'd immediately met with Detective Arantes. Within minutes, the police station came to life with activity, and reporters arrived to wait outside the building. But it wasn't until much later that she finally got word that the two vehicles had been stopped and the occupants apprehended.

When Filipe rejoined Catarina in the waiting room, worry filled his expression when his eyes landed on her. He drove her to the hospital, where she was admitted to the labor & delivery floor for overnight observation. The attending doctor explained to her how thirty-seven weeks was not too early to have a baby, and despite Catarina's concerns, the doctor had her hooked up to the monitors, with an IV in her arm and a promise that Dr. Paula would come see her in the morning.

After she rested and dehydrated, the early labor slowed down. As uncomfortable as she was with irregular contractions, the physical and emotional fatigue were greater, and she was able to sleep intermittently.

Filipe had left soon after she was admitted, and Catarina didn't know where he was. She would have to wait for him to return and tell her about Afonso.

The attending doctor came in right after the early breakfast, followed by a nurse. "How are you feeling today?" the doctor asked. He pulled out a stool and sat close to her bed. "Did you rest any?"

"A little," Catarina replied. "These false labor contractions are pretty tiring." Not to mention the dull pain she'd been having since the day before.

The doctor smiled. "They are tiring because they're not false labor. You're actually in labor. The real deal."

Catarina's jaw dropped, and her heart squeezed. "What? I'm not ready to have my baby." It was happening too soon.

The doctor chuckled. "Ready or not, the baby is coming. We've been monitoring you through the night, and even though the contractions have been irregular, you are in labor. I know I told you yesterday that Dr. Paula would be coming this morning, but she was delayed on a trip. She asked me to go ahead and check your progress so we can decide where to go from there."

After the exam, the doctor threw his gloves in the garbage. "You're dilated to four centimeters. I'm going to talk to Dr. Paula and see what she wants to do. In the meantime, do you need anything? Can we call anyone for you?"

Catarina sighed. "I think I left my tablet in my cousin's truck when he brought me yesterday. I don't have any numbers with me."

"What about your file? Do you have an emergency contact written there?" the nurse asked.

Had Catarina even put down an emergency number? "I can't remember."

"I'll go check for you," the nurse said.

She returned a few minutes later. "I looked at your file from the last time you were here, and I called the number under the emergency contact. He said he's on his way."

Catarina sat up in bed. "He did? Who did you call?"

"It said Afonso Cortez. Is it not right?"

Afonso was coming. Catarina swallowed the emotion in her throat and nodded. "No, it's right."

After the nurse left, Catarina wiped a tear from the corner of her eye. If he said he was coming, then he must be free to do so. She'd feared things would go wrong and he'd been detained again, but he was coming. She still had no idea where Afonso was traveling from and only hoped he could make it before the baby arrived.

Catarina waited all morning. The nurse brought her a light snack, but after lunch time, neither Afonso nor Dr. Paula had shown up.

After being in the same position all morning, Catarina asked to leave the bed for a respite. The contractions were still coming, bothersome and increasingly painful, but she needed a change. Waiting had worn out her patience: waiting for Dr. Paula, for Afonso, for the baby.

She dragged the IV stand and walked to the window with the nurse's help. A soft knock sounded at the door.

"Is it safe to come in?" a male voice asked.

Catarina covered her lips with her fingers. He was here. Afonso was here.

"It's safe," the nurse replied. She turned to Catarina and smiled. "Looks like your emergency contact finally made it."

The nurse opened the door to leave, and Afonso stepped in, timidly looking around. When he found the bed empty, he frowned.

"Afonso," Catarina said.

He looked in her direction, and a smile split his face, relief in his expression. In three large strides, he crossed the room to her side. "Catarina," he said in a low voice. Gingerly, he draped his arms around her shoulders and brought her closer to him.

Catarina inhaled deeply, relishing the embrace. She'd missed him so much.

Catarina let out a sigh. "You're here."

He pulled out to look at her. "Are you in pain? The nurse said you're in labor."

"I've been so worried about you," they both said at the same time.

Afonso chuckled and passed a hand through her hair. "You're the one having the baby. Truly, how are you?"

Catarina couldn't stop smiling. "I'm better now that you're here." A stronger contraction started in her lower back and she closed her eyes, hanging on to Afonso's arm. When it passed, she took a breath and reopened her eyes. "That was a big one. I think the baby knew I wanted you here before it started for real."

"Do you need to sit down?" His expression was full of concern. "What can I do for you?"

Catarina perched on the edge of the upholstered chair and held her breath as another wave of pain and pressure started. A bead of sweat rolled down her back.

"I'm getting the nurse," Afonso said. Worry laced his voice.

The nurse arrived within minutes with Afonso right behind.

"Okay, Catarina, let's get you back in bed and hooked to the monitor," the nurse said.

Catarina didn't protest.

With Afonso helping on one side and the nurse on the other, Catarina climbed back in bed. The nurse wrapped the monitor band around her belly and turned on the monitor as another contraction seized Catarina.

Catarina fell back against the pillows after it passed. Things were definitely moving quicker now.

Dr. Paula entered and pulled on a pair of gloves from the box on the counter. "Catarina, I heard your baby is ready to come." She eyed Afonso and smiled. "Awesome. The dad is here. Are you going to stick around?"

"Afonso Cortez. How are you?" Afonso didn't correct Dr. Paula.

"I'm great. Let me check Catarina and see how she's doing." She pulled a stool to the end of the bed, and the nurse dropped the footboard for better access.

Afonso turned toward the door, his neck red. "I'll come back in a few." Before Catarina had time to reply, he was out the door.

The nurse and Dr. Paula laughed. "Guys are so funny when it comes to childbirth," Dr. Paula said.

The doctor threw the gloves in the garbage after the exam. "You're at a tight six. We can wait to see how it progresses, and we can also help it along with some Pitocin which helps labor move faster."

Catarina's stomach churned. She'd already asked the other doctor, but she had to know. "So it's not too early for the baby to be born?"

The doctor consulted Catarina's chart. "You're past thirty-seven weeks, which is considered full term." She flipped through a few pages, then looked to Catarina. "You've been measuring small throughout your pregnancy, but your baby's last measurements showed consistent growth, and he or she looks to be doing great." She smiled. "Everything will be fine."

Catarina released the breath she'd been holding in and nodded. "If you say so."

Dr. Paula patted Catarina's leg. "I definitely say so." She looked back through the chart. "We talked about you getting an epidural. Are you still i nterested?"

"Yes, please," Catarina replied without hesitation.

"All right then. I'll get the anesthesiologist to come first. I'll check back with you soon to decide about the Pitocin."

The anesthesiologist came thirty minutes later, and while the experience of receiving the epidural was less fun than Catarina had hoped, the prospect of unmedicated labor was something she didn't want to deal with.

Afonso returned half an hour after that.

"You're back," Catarina said.

"I'm back." He smiled and handed her a paper gift bag. "I got you a few things."

She peeked inside. "My tablet." It was actually Filipe's tablet, but she'd been using it for a while.

"Filipe asked me to return it."

Inside the bag there was also a pair of white socks, a packet of mint gum, a pen and a small pad, and her favorite brand of flavored water. "Thank you, Afonso. This is so thoughtful."

His neck reddened. "I know you didn't get the chance to bring anything, but Luciana said she'll pack a bag for you when she gets here."

"Did you call her?"

"Yes, she's driving to Porto to bring your parents, possibly later today or tomorrow morning. Tiago said he'll come on Saturday with your grandma and aunts."

"How did you talk to Tiago?"

He nodded. "I met him, plus your dad, granddad, and some other cousins, aunts, and uncles."

"How did that happen? You need to tell me everything." She still didn't know what had happened after Afonso had left with Anabela's brother.

Afonso chuckled. "Are you up for it?"

"I got the epidural." Catarina smiled. "Now I'm just waiting."

Afonso stood and watched the monitor to the side of the bed. "Your contractions have picked up quite a bit."

Catarina craned her neck. "Really?"

He gestured at the screen. "Look at the peaks."

"I can't feel anything. It's great." Thank goodness for modern medicine. "Start with what happened after you left the house."

Afonso sat back down. "I tried to speed every time I saw another vehicle, hoping someone would report us, or a highway patrol car would pull us over, but Anabela's brother wouldn't let me. I kept trying to talk him out of it, which didn't work either. Fortunately we ran out of gas, so we had to stop to fill up, and when we were about to leave, three patrol cars cut us off."

"What about Anabela?"

"She was pulled over for speeding, and when they ran her driver's license, the warrant for her arrest came up."

Dr. Paula and two nurses entered the room. Catarina looked up in surprise. She'd been so focused on listening to Afonso that, for a moment, she'd almost forgotten the baby was coming soon.

"Let's see if you're ready," the doctor said.

Afonso stood to leave again, but this time Catarina latched on to his hand, holding him in place. The nurses moved to each side of Catarina, and one of them draped a sheet from Catarina's belly to her knees. The other dropped the footboard and lifted the stirrups. Afonso looked at Catarina, then squeezed her fingers. He sat back down and scooted his chair closer to the head of the bed. The nurses bent Catarina's legs at the knee, holding them in position for the exam. Afonso focused on Catarina's face, blushing furiously in his attempt to give her privacy.

Dr. Paula peeked over the sheet. "You're dilated to ten, one hundred percent effaced, and your contractions are coming in every two minutes. When the next contraction starts, I want you to push."

Catarina's eyes widened. "Already? I can't feel anything. How do I know when to push?" This was happening too fast. She still hadn't wrapped her brain around the idea of having her baby at thirty-seven weeks, and now the baby was coming.

"We'll tell you when to push. When we count to

ten, I want you to hold in your breath and bear down through the push until we stop counting."

Catarina did as they told her. One push after another, through each count of ten, holding on to Afonso's hand as if she could get the strength she needed from him. He'd migrated closer to her, his face almost sharing the same pillow, whispering words of encouragement, but an hour and a half later Catarina was still pushing.

After another count to ten, she fell back against the pillow. "I can't do this," she panted. She was so tired; so ready to have her baby and had no strength left.

Afonso wiped the sweat from her forehead with a cool washcloth and brought an ice chip to her lips. She sucked on it, lacking the stamina for more.

The nurses and doctor gave her a few minutes of reprieve, their worried expressions weighing on her as they talked in hushed tones.

When the word *cesarean* reached her ears, she shook her head. "No, not that." She panted. "Let me try again."

Dr. Paula and both nurses rushed to their former positions. Afonso braced himself at her side, holding on to her hand and forearm. "You can do it, Catarina," he said softly in her ear.

The gentle words gave her courage. If Afonso said it, it must be true, because Afonso never lied. He was the most honest person she knew, and she believed him. She could do it.

They started counting again, and Catarina scrunched her eyes. She bore down, giving her all. In her mind she repeated *I can do it, I can do it*, Afonso's words echoing along with hers. Catarina concentrated on his strong hand holding hers, on the warmth of his body next to hers as her own body trembled with the hardest thing she'd ever had to do. She pushed and pushed until she ran out of breath. Once, twice, three times she pushed. At last, with a final thrust, the baby was out, and Catarina fell back, the wave of relief washing through her. A tiny cry rent the air, and Catarina smiled through her tears. Her baby was born.

Dr. Paula stood and, in a swift movement, the nurse placed a warm blanket on Catarina's chest and the doctor gently passed the squirming infant onto Catarina's welcoming body.

"Congratulations, Catarina. It's a girl."

Catarina half sobbed, half laughed as she watched her daughter, flailing fists and angry red face, complaining at the top of her lungs. The nurses pulled the blanket tighter on the baby, and Catarina's arms went around her daughter.

"I have a daughter," she said to Afonso. His eyes were red and suspiciously wet, and a wide grin lit his face.

He bent closer and kissed her forehead, and she felt his tears against her skin. "Well done, Catarina. Well done."

Her daughter was born.

Afonso knocked softly, and Catarina waved him in. "Afonso, you're here."

"I'm sorry I'm late." Between getting the house ready for guests and giving Catarina's family time to visit with her, he'd finally arrived at the hospital after visiting hours.

The room was semidark, with the peripheral lights on and a fluorescent bulb that shone from the wall over the bed. Catarina straightened and smiled. He'd missed her smile so much. He carried a pink Mylar balloon and one long-stemmed rose in a single vase, which he set down on the free-standing tray.

Catarina sat on the bed with a small bundle in her arms. "How did you get in after hours?"

He pulled a chair closer to the bed. "I was ready to bribe the nurse, but she recognized me from before."

"And they still think you're the father, don't they?"

He shrugged. "I didn't feel like correcting them." What would Catarina say if he offered to be her baby's father?

Before sitting down, he brushed a kiss on Catarina's forehead. Her eyes softened, and he wished he could take her in his arms and give her a real kiss. In due time, preferably sooner than later.

Catarina scooted to the side and shifted the baby from her arms to the mattress, where Afonso could see her better.

"She looks so different already," Afonso said. It had been a day since the baby's birth, and he noted the changes.

Catarina chuckled. "She was pretty mad when she was born, all red and puffy." She loosened the blanket and uncovered the baby's feet. "I love her little feet. Actually, I love all her little parts." The smile on Catarina's face showed all the love she had for her daughter.

"Do you have a name for her yet?"

"Carlota Beatriz." She looked up to Afonso, expectantly.

"Wasn't there a princess named Carlota?"

"Was there?"

He nodded. "I'm pretty sure there was. I like it. A royal name for a little princess."

They watched the baby as she slept peacefully between them, and Afonso burned the moment in his mind and willed it to last forever. Just the three of them together. He'd give everything to get his wish. "I think she looks like you."

"You really think so?" Catarina glanced at him and then back at the baby.

"That little nose is definitely all yours."

Catarina's lips stretched into a small smile. "This is going to sound petty, but I've been so worried she'd look more like Juan-Carlos." She didn't say *like her husband* or *like Carlota's dad*, and Afonso could have kissed her right that moment, hoping it meant she was moving on and looking to the future. A future that included him.

"You didn't get to finish telling me what happened after the highway patrol cars caught you and Anabela's brother," Catarina said.

"They had the license plate for the truck, so they knew it was the vehicle they were looking for. Filipe said you gave the plate number to the police? I didn't know you had it memorized." He still didn't know all the details of what had happened after he was forced to drive with Anabela's brother.

"I didn't. When you left, I went to the sliding door and told Anabela I was watching you leave. But I fogged up the glass and wrote the license number down. I didn't trust myself to memorize it." She shrugged.

"But how did Anabela let you go?"

Catarina's mouth rose in a little smile. "I pretended I was in labor, and she left. She smashed my phone on her way out, and I called the Silvas from the tablet. They drove me to Castelo Branco."

Afonso watched her, the admiration growing in his chest. "You are amazing, you know that?" Afonso rested a hand on her forearm. "Here you are in labor, and you outsmart the woman who was holding you hostage and then go to the police before you go to the hospital, which you didn't even have to do."

"Of course I had to do it." Her expression hardened. "I wasn't going to let her get away with ruining the life of the man I—" She stopped short. "I just couldn't."

His breath hitched. Did she almost say what he thought she meant? Catarina had hinted before about her feelings for him, but they hadn't had the chance to talk about it since then. His heart jumped in his chest as a cautiously joyous anticipation took root in it.

Catarina went on. "I couldn't let her send you to prison for something that wasn't your fault. And she had a bomb planned, didn't she?"

Afonso nodded, continuing the conversation, but really wanting to get to the part he had in mind. "She did. It was in a Porto warehouse. That's why it took longer for me to return. After they got Anabela, we were all brought in for questioning. Matias and Filipe came to the station and registered their depositions, and that took a while." He'd made sure there was enough evidence on record to charge Anabela and her brother. "Afterward, Matias took me to his apartment for a shower and a change of clothes, and we had an early breakfast at your grandparents', where I met some of your family."

"Why did Anabela do all of it?" Catarina asked.

"It turns out that Anabela's father worked for Senhor Valadares, and he died in the same accident that killed Vanessa's mother. Anabela always blamed it on the company and grew up resentful. She used her mother's maiden name to get a job on the ship and planned for a chance to get even." As more details had emerged about Anabela, Afonso had struggled to know he'd been a willing part in her plan last year. His lack of judgment had been tremendous, and he'd learned his lesson the hard way.

The baby flinched in her sleep, and Catarina tightened the blanket around her. "I'm just glad that it's over."

"It is. They've both been arraigned and will be incarcerated while they await trial." Afonso was ready to move on and truly put his past behind him. He took a breath, gathering the courage to say what he should have said a long time ago.

Catarina looked to Afonso, then back down to the baby. "There's something I have to tell you."

Her tone was serious, with a twinge of hesitancy, and Afonso turned to her.

"It's something I found out when Luciana came to see me after my fall." Catarina took a breath. "I've had time to think today. I want to come clean and tell you everything I've held back from you."

A knot twisted in his chest. Where was she going with this?

"Luciana got curious about you being a pianist, and she Googled your name. And as the links and pictures loaded, she found some from when you played in Barcelona." She paused and breathed in, as if to get courage to go on. "There was one picture in particular, taken after a concert at the opera house, with the mayor and the maestro, and, of course, you in the middle, and to the other side, one of the symphony patrons and his wife."

Afonso took her closest hand in his, anticipating what she was going to say.

"That patron was Juan-Carlos, and the wife was me." She sniffled. "I'm that Dulce Vega that Anabela mentioned. His name was Juan-Carlos de Aragón y Vega, and Dulce was the name he gave me." She paused and swallowed." I don't remember meeting you, Afonso. I was in such a dark place at that time. I'd just found out he'd had another affair, and there I was, having to pose next to him pretending everything was okay." She wiped the tears on her face and took a fortifying breath. "I don't even have the courage to show it to you, but it's on the internet, with a link to the Barcelona newspaper. I'm sure you can find it easily."

Afonso traced a circle with his thumb on the back of her hand. "I know, Catarina." It was his turn to confess. "I remember that photo op. When I arrived at Sunset Manor, I didn't recognize you right away, but you seemed familiar. It was the reason I asked if we'd met before. You looked so different from when you'd been with him, and I wasn't sure."

She blushed. "I was a different person back then."

"I looked up your husband's name a few months ago after Filipe said something in passing. I found out Juan-Carlos' family is from Barcelona and eventually I saw that picture too." He'd been shocked to see it. "I remember meeting that young woman and thinking how sad her eyes were." He'd thought about her for days.

"You never said anything." Catarina pulled her hand and covered her face. "I can't even imagine what you must think of me, all the lies I told, every-thing I held back from you."

Afonso reached for her hand again. "I never said anything because I wanted to avoid this—you blaming yourself for something that was not completely your fault. You don't have to be ashamed of your past, Cata-rina. You're not that person anymore." Just thinking about what she had gone through with that man, it made him sick. "You're so brave, and you've come so far. You even tricked Anabela and your quick thinking was instrumental in bringing her down." He reached a finger and touched the baby's hair with a gentle stroke. "And look what you've done. She's so beautiful."

Catarina placed her fingers on the baby's hands and smiled through her tears. "She is, isn't she? So beautiful and perfect. What did I do to deserve her?" She sighed. "I don't even know what I'm going to do when I leave the hospital."

"For now, we're still at the manor house. Your cousins are setting up a nursery in the sitting area of your suite." He brought a finger to his lips. "Shh, it's a surprise. Don't tell them I told you."

She mimicked the gesture. "I'll be surprised. Is Filipe selling Sunset Manor then?"

"He's seriously thinking about it. The Silvas decided to retire and with the end of my contract in a couple of weeks, Filipe said he might not wait till spring to sell. He hasn't listed it yet, but he's had some private offers, and he's having the lawyers go over them."

"I have mixed feelings about that place." She sighed, and her voice turned wistful. "I'm pretty sure I won't miss living so far away from everything, but I have lots of fond memories."

"Me too." They'd met at Sunset Manor, and that was something he'd never forget.

Catarina bit her lip. "What are your plans now that you're almost done with your contract? Do you know where you're going next?"

Afonso gathered his courage. This was it. Please, don't let him botch it. "My plans are a bit flexible, but I've been looking at this place here in town." He pulled his phone from his pocket and, minding the sleeping baby, leaned closer to Catarina, showing her the screen as he swiped through the pictures. "I found this apartment. Well, it's actually a small two-story building. The ground floor has a garage that spans the length of the house with lots of storage space, plus a backyard. It's located ten to fifteen minutes from downtown, depending on the traffic. The apartment is on the first floor. It's a three-bedroom, one and a half baths, large kitchen and dining room, plus a family room with an office nook. It's in good condition and the seller is motivated. It just needs a good cleaning and some fresh paint." He was talking too fast, and he paused to inhale. "What do you think?"

Catarina straightened and took the baby in her arms, leaning away from him. "It's nice. You'll have lots of space, for sure. The price looks good too."

A bead of sweat rolled down the back of his neck. He wasn't explaining things right, and Catarina was pulling away from him already. "There was a reward attached to Anabela's capture, and with the final pay from working at Sunset Manor coming in, it would be a good investment. As for the extra space, I thought— I thought—like you said, there's so much room for just one person. What are your plans?" he blurted. This conversation was not going the way he'd imagined.

Catarina frowned. "I don't know what my plans are yet. My parents asked me if I'd like to return to Porto. It would be nice to have family close by and to raise Carlota around them." She worried her bottom lip, watching the baby. "There's so much to consider."

How could he compete with her family when there was only one of him? If she wanted to go to Porto, he'd follow her there, but he had to find out what she thought of his plan first. "You know, I'm looking for someone to share the house with. If you wanted to stay in Castelo Branco," he added. Why was this so hard? The more he said, the harder it got.

"Are you asking me to share a house with you?"

"I was thinking more like a roommate."

"A roommate?" Her voice took on an incredulous tone. "I just had a baby. What kind of proposition is that?" She shifted the baby into the crook of her arm, her expression tight and her eyes cast down.

Afonso stood, slipped his phone into his pocket, and knelt on the floor by the bed, taking her free

256

hand into both of his. "It's a proposal, and I'm making a mess of it."

Catarina's eyes widened, and her chin dropped in surprise.

"I'm asking you to marry me, Catarina." Relief came over him at finally saying what he really had wanted to say for too long. "I'm so nervous, I can't even get the right words out, but I love you so much, and I don't want to lose you. Neither of you." From his other pocket, he drew a square box and opened the lid. A simple white-gold band with three tiny diamonds.

Catarina's eyes filled with tears, and she choked on a sob. She tugged at his hands, and that was all the encouragement he needed. Afonso rose and sat next to her on the bed, placing his arms around her and the baby, his heart filled with more love than he ever thought possible.

Catarina buried her face in his neck and kissed him there. "I love you too, Afonso," she whispered in his ear. "I'm so glad you came to Sunset Manor."

He closed his eyes and savored the closeness between them. Hope surged inside him. "Is that a yes?"

She leaned back to look at him, and the corner of her mouth raised in a teasing smile. "That depends— do you want a roommate or a wife?"

"Definitely a wife."

"Then my answer is yes."

Afonso slipped the ring onto her finger, then he reached a hand behind her neck and pulled Catarina closer, covering her lips with his mouth and pouring all his love into the gesture.

She would never doubt his love.

EPILOGUE

*T*he day rose clear and cold, and the frost clinging to the winter-dormant roses shone in the early gray sunlight. In the valley below, the village of Sete Fontes hid behind a layer of gossamer fog.

Catarina smiled with a contented sigh at the view from her bedroom. So much had changed since she'd arrived in the early spring, so much would change from today.

In the bassinet by her bed, Carlota finally slept after being awake for half the night. Catarina would have to wake her in a few hours to get her ready for the christening, but for now she enjoyed the quiet.

Her phone chirped with a text from Afonso. **Let me in?**

She walked to the door and noiselessly turned the handle. He still wore his pajama bottoms and an old

259

T-shirt. Catarina let him pass and closed the door behind him, glad he'd oiled the hinges last week.

"What are you doing here? If my mom and aunts catch you…" she whispered.

He laughed quietly and slipped an arm around her waist, intent clear in his eyes.

The sound of a car crawling up the drive interrupted them and brought them to the window. "Do you think it's Luciana?" Catarina asked. Everyone else who was coming had arrived the day before, but Luciana had been on a job in New York, stranded over the Christmas season after a snowstorm.

In the bassinet, Carlota squirmed, and Catarina sagged against Afonso. "She's such a light sleeper."

He brushed a kiss on her cheek. "Go meet your cousin. I'll watch Carlota."

Catarina returned the kiss on the cheek. "Don't let my mom see you leave."

He chuckled. "I'll come downstairs after I change Carlota's diaper."

When Catarina arrived in the kitchen, Luciana stood at the espresso machine. "You came," Catarina said.

Luciana smiled and hugged Catarina. "I wouldn't have missed this for the world."

"I thought you were still in New York."

"I managed to catch a flight last night. I arrived in Lisbon and drove straight here."

Catarina's eyes widened. "You must be so tired."

Luciana dropped a spoonful of sugar in the small cup

and stirred. "That's what the espresso is for. I'll catch a nap after the christening. There'll be time, right?"

"Plenty of time. The christening is at eleven at the village church. We'll have a light lunch, and the wedding is here at five in the afternoon."

Luciana smiled. "Look at you, so cool and collected. Aren't you nervous at all?"

"Excited, but not nervous. Now tell me, how did the project go in New York?"

"It went well." Luciana sipped slowly. "Better than I expected."

"Where did you stay, and what did you do while you were waiting for the airport to open again?"

Luciana finished her coffee. "I promise I'll tell you everything, but not today." She walked to the table and reached inside her large purse. "I did have the time to finish my goddaughter's outfit. It's in here somewhere."

Carlota would wear the Romano christening gown for the ceremony and formal pictures, and Catarina would change her from that when they returned from the church.

"Is it true Knox proposed to Jacinta on Christmas Eve?" Luciana asked as she withdrew items from her purse.

"It's true. They're engaged."

"Finally. I don't know what took him so long. Hope they set a date soon."

Catarina drew the milk from the refrigerator. "They already did. Jacinta said she's waited enough and they don't need a long engagement."

"Good for her. We'll have two Romano weddings this year."

"Three, with Matias and Vanessa."

"Ha, here it is." Luciana placed a small bundle on the table and unwrapped it. A two-piece outfit of pure white yarn with pink embellishments nestled inside. "Do you think it'll fit her?"

Catarina fingered it reverently. "She's a chubbers, but I'll make it fit. This is exquisite, Luciana. Obrigada."

Just then, the complaints of a grumpy baby sounded from the door. Afonso entered the kitchen holding Carlota in the crook of his arm. "Someone's ready for breakfast, mamã."

"I'll warm up the bottle," Catarina said.

Luciana stepped forward and took the baby from him. "Oh my goodness. She's changed so much. So adorable." She cooed at Carlota. "Look how big you are."

"Glad you made it, Luciana. We heard you had an adventure in America," Afonso teased.

Luciana chuckled lightly. "What I want to know is why you guys couldn't wait till spring to get married. It's so cold today."

The way she sidestepped the question, Luciana had a story there, but Catarina would have to put it aside for now.

Afonso exchanged a look with her, and she nodded at him to reply.

"We wanted to start the new year as a family," he

said. "No point in waiting on account of the weather. What better day to symbolize a new beginning?"

Catarina handed the warmed bottle to Luciana, much to Carlota's happiness.

Luciana sat down, gazing at the baby for a moment, then looked up between Catarina and Afonso. "How did you manage to convince a magistrate to perform the wedding on a holiday?"

Afonso and Catarina sat next to each other. Afonso winked. "I had some connections that Filipe set me up with."

Carlota sighed in contentment, and Luciana returned her attention to the baby. "Pardon my nosiness. You guys can tell me it's none of my business. But what about the legal procedures concerning this little lady? I'm assuming Afonso is adopting her. How long will that take?"

Afonso brought an arm around Catarina's shoulders, and she leaned into him with a smile. She lowered her voice. "He won't be adopting."

Luciana snapped up to them, frowning.

"I'm Carlota's legal father," Afonso added.

"We had Carlota registered with Afonso as the father. As far as the registrar in Castelo Branco knows, Carlota is our daughter."

"That's awesome." Luciana nodded at them. "I'm really glad for you both." She propped the baby on her shoulder, and Carlota burped.

Afonso stood and took Catarina's hand in his. "It looks like nobody else is up yet, and you're feeding our daughter, so I'm taking advantage to have a moment with my bride."

Luciana winked at them. "Go ahead. I'll cover for you if anyone shows up."

Afonso led Catarina through the house, past the entry hall, and to the music room. He drew open the heavy wood shutters, from where the rose garden was visible.

"Are you trying to remind me of where we met?" she asked.

Afonso didn't reply. Instead, he slipped his arms around her waist and pulled her close, claiming her lips to his, slowly, deliberately, a deep sensuous kiss that stole all the air from her chest.

When he was done, he touched his lips to the spot on her neck below her ear. "Next time I kiss you like this, we'll be married," he whispered. The warm gleam in his eyes promised much more than a kiss.

The small hairs on her neck raised, and Catarina melted into him. She took a deep breath and grabbed on to his arms, her legs unstable and her knees shaky. "Only twelve more hours."

"Twelve hours seems like forever," he said with a hint of impatience.

"After today, it will be for always," she reminded him.

Afonso's mouth curved in a confident smile. "Forever is worth waiting for."

DEAR READER

𝒯hank you so much for reading Afonso and Catarina's story, *Love Me at Sunset*. I hope you've enjoyed reading it as much as I enjoyed writing it. You may learn more about them and their story on Pinterest.

Please consider leaving a review on Amazon and Goodreads. This is the best way to support me as an author.

For news of upcoming books and promotions, join my readers club.

I love to hear from readers! You can email me at lucinda@lucindawhitney.com.

Thank you!

Want to find out how Matias and Vanessa met? Turn the page to read *Meet Me at Sunrise*.

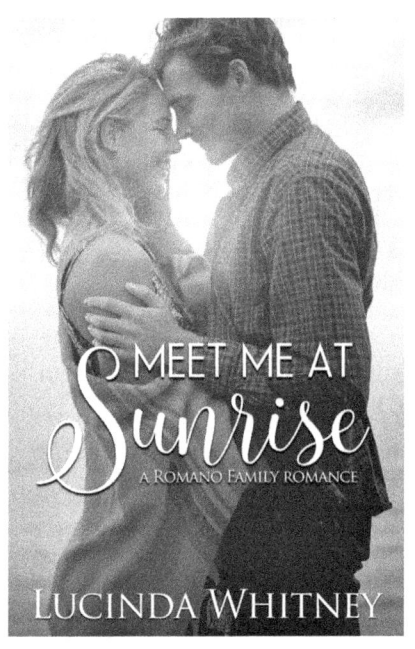

Read Matias and Vanessa's story
in *Meet Me at Sunrise*.

CHAPTER ONE

*T*his was a bad idea. Why had she let Grandfather talk her into this trip?

Vanessa stopped at the entrance of the ship's formal dining room and gazed around. Outside the panoramic windows, the city of Porto inched up the hill from the docks on the other side of the river, the buildings and roofs and church towers competing for space unsuccessfully. Myriad lights shone against the night sky and spilled in reflective ribbons on the water's surface. In its architectural disorganization, there was a beauty that called to her. It was a city so unlike the ones she was used to. Much of Portugal was still a mystery to her.

Inside, the passengers sat in groups of eight at round tables, and waiters in white coats flitted between them with silver platters and bottles of wine. Everything in the room spoke of elegance and luxury, from the furniture and dark wood trim to the impeccably white tablecloths and fresh-cut flowers to the damask draperies drawn back with silver ropes and the pianist undulating at the baby grand.

She'd barely looked at the pamphlets Grandfather had sent her and was not prepared for the real-life opulence before her. She—the Kansas girl who preferred well-worn jeans and flip-flops to dresses and high heels—aboard the *MS Princess Catarina,* the crown jewel in Grandfather's fleet of luxury river ships. How long until someone recognized she didn't belong here?

A very bad idea indeed.

At least she was by herself. She'd managed to convince Grandfather she didn't need the bodyguard he'd planned to send with her. As president of a multi-million-dollar company, he was the one who needed bodyguards. She was just an American girl on her own, and nobody knew of her yet. Besides, what could possibly go wrong on a small cruise ship?

Inside her clutch, her phone rang. It was probably Dad. Again. He'd insisted on being able to contact her throughout the trip and had prearranged a new plan with Verizon. He'd have to wait until tomorrow to talk to her.

An appetizing scent reached her nose. Roasted pork, rosemary potatoes, and something else she couldn't identify. Vanessa was late to dinner and she had missed the "Welcome Aboard" cocktail party.

The light breakfast from this morning was only a memory by now. Her stomach rumbled.

The maître d' appeared at her elbow. "May I have your name, please?"

Vanessa turned to him, grateful that English was the official language aboard. "Vanessa Clark. Is it open seating?" she asked, while he checked the list in front of him.

"Not for you, Miss Clark. Please follow me."

As he cut a path to the center of the dining room, Vanessa ignored the urge to smooth her dress and held on to her sequined clutch instead, carefully stepping on the gleaming wood floor and willing herself not to trip on her strappy sandals.

Was it her imagination or did most people pause to look at her? The conversations and clinking of silverware against the porcelain dishes continued on around them, as a few of the passengers darted their eyes at her. This was karma for being the last one to arrive at dinner. For someone who didn't like attention, she sure had a lot of it now.

The maître d' pulled out a chair next to a dark-haired man in a black uniform. He was clean-shaven and appeared to be in his early thirties, with an air of confidence that drew her attention. Who was he and what did he do?

The man stood and nodded at her. "Good evening, Miss Clark."

Her eyes widened for a moment. How did he know who she was?

He didn't smile openly, but his mouth curved

into a pleasant expression, and Vanessa's lips rose in response.

"I'm glad you made it." His voice was deep and lightly accented, and his arresting brown eyes held hers for a moment longer than good manners called for.

After an awkward pause, they sat down and Vanessa dragged the bib-size napkin onto her lap, looking away from him and realizing the other guests at the table were staring at her. She drew a quick breath. There was a spotlight directly above, and the heat from it bore a hole in her head. Was the air conditioning even on? Goodness, he was just a man, and not even the most attractive one she'd ever met. Why the sudden discomfort?

"Is this your lovely wife, Captain?" The lady across from them asked.

Captain? Wife? Vanessa turned to the man, noting for the first time the white stripes on his sleeves. "I'm sorry, I didn't realize you were the captain." Her cheeks heated at the mistake. She was seated to the captain's right, without a doubt arranged by Grandfather.

He cleared his throat. "She is lovely but no, not my wife." He shrugged in a self-deprecating manner, and the other passengers at the table chuckled lightly.

He turned to her. "I'm Captain Romano, Miss Clark." He then addressed the other passengers who shared their table. "Allow me to introduce Miss Clark, from the United States of America." He started at his left and went around the table. "Dr. and Mrs. Whitehead, from the UK; Mr. and Mrs. Grantham, also from the UK; and Mr. and Mrs. Grosse, from Germany."

Vanessa nodded and smiled politely at them before they returned to their meals.

"Miss Clark, I apologize for the blunder," one of the English ladies said. "But there was an empty chair next to the captain and he seemed to have been waiting for you." She looked between Vanessa and Captain Romano. "And you two make such a striking couple."

Vanessa's cheeks reddened, the curse of a light complexion, courtesy of Dad's Scandinavian ancestry.

"I haven't had the pleasure of meeting Miss Clark until now," the captain said.

Vanessa nodded. "Yes, what he said." She cringed inside. Why couldn't she come up with an appropriate reply when she needed one?

She busied herself with the perfectly seasoned potatoes on her plate instead. If she nodded and looked interested in the conversations around her, maybe she wouldn't have to say too much and could save herself from any more embarrassing responses.

"What state are you from, Miss Clark?" the German man asked, his accent evidence of his origins.

Vanessa paused to look at him. "I'm from Kansas."

His forehead wrinkled and he looked at his wife who gave him a small shrug.

"It's in the middle of the country. You know, lots of farming and fields, *The Wizard of Oz* and tornadoes," she explained, her words running together.

273

They nodded in understanding. Maybe she should stop talking now.

Vanessa waited for more questions, but thankfully none came, and she slowly let out a small breath of relief as the attention shifted from her.

One of the English men put his fork down. "Captain Romano, is Chef Teresa still on your crew?"

The captain smiled. "She certainly is. In fact, I have the same exact crew as last year." The pride in his voice was unmistakable.

Was this a common occurrence, to ask after the crew? Her knowledge of cruise etiquette was ridiculously poor despite what she'd read before coming, and even though Grandfather owned the vessel.

The questions continued for the rest of the meal, keeping the captain busy as he gave everyone his attention. How did he find the time to eat? His patience was admirable.

As the courses changed, the captain picked up the bottle of red wine, and Vanessa watched him pour a glass of the burgundy liquid for her. She thanked him and brought the glass to her lips, tasting a drop too small to swallow. The flavor was foreign to her, and she chased it down with a large gulp of the mineral water from the other tall glass in front of her. As she set the glass down, her hand trembled, and she tightened her grip on the stem until the base touched the table. How much longer until she could take refuge in her cabin?

As another waiter slipped a plate with the next

course in front of her, she looked casually to the neighboring tables.

Couples. All the passengers sitting in the dining room were couples. Middle-aged and senior couples eating and talking and laughing. She couldn't find another person close to her age among the hundred and thirty passengers. The growing uneasiness tightened in her chest, and she suppressed a sigh. What had Grandfather done, sticking her on a fancy river cruise with the upper crust of Europe?

Captain Romano leaned in her direction. "Is everything all right, Miss Clark?"

Vanessa's tongue stuck to her palate, and she took another drink of the barely cold water. "Please, call me Vanessa, Captain." She raised her eyes to him. "Have you met my grandfather?"

One of the waiters came to the captain and handed him a small card. He tucked it in his pocket and then turned to the rest of the table. "Excuse me, ladies and gentlemen. I am needed elsewhere for a moment."

As he stood, he made eye contact with Vanessa. "Excuse me, Miss Clark," he said to her.

Vanessa nodded in response, not knowing what else to say. Why did he single her out?

What an unfortunate time for him to leave, and how disappointing for her. Now she'd have to wait for another chance to ask him about Grandfather.

Matias Romano looked around for the cruise director. When he spotted her across the room chatting with a group of passengers, he rose and excused himself from the last table. He always took the time to greet all the passengers after dinner and he wouldn't start making exceptions on this trip. But he could leave the rest of the evening in Anabela Rialto's capable hands. Mingling and interacting with the passengers were some of her duties, and Matias had observed over the last few trips and she seemed to enjoy that part of her job.

He had other matters to think about. Like Miss Vanessa Clark. They hadn't had a chance to talk in private at the table, and she had left the dining room abruptly after the dessert course was cleared, not even waiting for the after-dinner espresso to be served. If she had returned to her cabin, he'd have to talk to her some other time. But leaving her question unanswered wasn't ideal, and he felt obligated to set a friendly tone between them.

He quickly exited through the main lobby and climbed the stairs to the sun deck. He stopped short before reaching the bridge. There she was, to the starboard side, leaning casually by the railing, looking out to the city on the other side of the river. Her face was in profile, and her long blonde hair blew gently in the breeze. It was a lovely scene and she was a lovely woman, but there was nothing more to it.

So what if he was partial to blondes? A pretty face didn't hold much interest for him when she'd behaved so snobbishly at dinner. She had picked at her food and barely spoken to any of the other passengers, gazing around the room with an air of aloofness instead. As the only granddaughter of the company's president, she was probably used to the royal treatment, but that didn't give her the right to look down on the other passengers. Suddenly, talking to her wasn't a pressing matter anymore.

Why had he agreed to António Valadares's hare-brained idea? Sure, he could hardly deny any request from the president of the entire fleet of river cruise ships, but acting as a personal guide to his heiress granddaughter was not in Matias's job description. He should have said no, plain and simple. He was the captain, not a babysitter to a young woman who had everything. But his sense of duty had prevailed instead, as it usually did. There was more at stake than his personal preferences. Senhor Valadares had hinted at a problem with the future of the company, but Matias wasn't sure how it tied to the granddaughter.

Matias slowed down and squared his shoulders, letting out a slow breath. A hint of anticipation flared up, and he quickly squelched it, annoyed with himself at the twinge of attraction that sparked for a second too long. He only needed to talk to her. Nothing more.

She stood barefoot, her high-heeled sandals lying on their sides, her small purse next to them. Matias resisted the urge to return them to her and shoved his hands in his pants' pockets. He cleared his throat to greet her, but she spoke first.

"How many times have you made this trip, Captain?"

"Quite a few, Miss Clark." He faced the city as she did.

This was his seventeenth time up the river on this particular route. He knew because he'd been recording all his trips—not only the cruises but also the fishing and stocking ones—since he'd boarded his first boat as a deck hand at the age of fourteen. There were official records as well but he didn't like admitting to that level of precision and mostly kept the exact number to himself. "Miss Clark—"

She interrupted him. "And just how long have you been working for this company?"

Matias turned to her. "Is there a reason to your questioning, Miss Clark?" He kept his tone level and even, but his fingers tightened around the key ring inside his right pocket. What was it about this woman? He'd barely met her, and already she set him on edge in a way no one else had in his recent memory.

She leaned away from the railing and turned partially to him. "Just trying to determine how well you know my grandfather."

"Yes, you asked me that earlier. I'm sorry I didn't reply." They'd been interrupted by another passenger needing help, as he was so often during meals.

Matias took a quick breath and braced himself for

more questions. He didn't know what to expect from her and it made him uneasy. The reaction was new to him, but she was more than a simple passenger, and it would serve him well not to forget the connections she had. "I have met your grandfather on several occasions since I started working at the company."

She turned away from him and let out a long sigh. "Probably more times than I have." Her words came out quick and low, and maybe not intended for him to hear.

"Is there a problem?" He paused and made eye contact.

"Not a problem exactly." She looked away and drummed her fingers along the rail.

"Is there something you're not happy with, Miss Clark?" They hadn't even departed, and already she had complaints. Usually he left the passenger-related matters to his cruise director, but not this one. She was in his hands, whether he liked it or not. "I know you're probably used to more personal service, but if you give us a chance, you might be pleasantly surprised."

Miss Clark's eyebrows knit in a scowl, but she didn't comment right away. After a long moment, she asked, "Are all the cabins as large as mine?"

"Excuse me?"

"The cabin assigned to me. Is that the standard cabin size?" She fidgeted with a length of hair, and when his eyes turned to it, she dropped it and flicked it behind her back.

The gesture lasted only a few seconds, but he lost his train of thought as it latched onto the woman in front of him. Matias struggled to resume their strange conversation. "Actually," he shook his head. "Uh, no. Your cabin is one of two deluxe cabins on the ship. We refer to them as the grand cabins, and they're reserved for our VIP passengers."

It was her turn to shake her head. "He did it, didn't he? He put me in that cabin?"

This conversation was turning more bizarre each minute. "If there's a problem with your cabin, I'll ask Miss Rialto to look into it. She's our cruise director, and I'll introduce you if you haven't had the chance to meet her. Your grandfather requested you stay in that particular cabin since it's the largest and best on the ship, and I have an obligation—"

Her eyes went wide. "Obligation? Obligation to what?"

Not to what, to whom. Her, to be exact. Matias didn't reply.

"To me, isn't it? You were going to say you have an obligation to me, weren't you?"

Matias flinched at her words and the way she'd read his mind. He rubbed his forehead. "It's not like how you make it sound." He forced his eyes to her. "Yes, I have an obligation toward you but it's the obligation I have toward all the passengers on board as well as my crew. I am the captain, after all."

Her shoulders relaxed a fraction, and Matias pressed on. "Your grandfather only wanted to make sure you have the best experience on this trip and even you can't fault him for that." Matias knew from his own research that she was his only granddaughter.

"I'm sure he did." She shook her head lightly, and her shoulders slumped even more, as if something weighed on her. "I don't need a babysitter, Captain. In case you haven't noticed, I'm a grown woman."

He'd noticed all right. More than he wished to, but he wouldn't be telling her that.

"Did he tell you why he wanted me to take this trip?" she asked.

Matias fumbled to find a reply and she waved him off. "That's okay, I don't want to know what he said. There's enough drama as it is."

It was family drama and he should stay out it. Well, most of it. He was already involved.

After a moment, she straightened and met his eyes. "At what time does the boat leave tomorrow?"

"The ship departs after lunch." He emphasized the word to correct her. It certainly wasn't a boat. "There's a guided excursion in the morning."

She bent to pick up her shoes and tucked the purse under her arm. "What are the rules about leaving?"

"Any time the ship is docked, you can leave at your leisure. But if you don't make it back before departure, we can't hold it for you."

She nodded. "That's only fair."

As she walked past him, he cleared his throat.

"Nobody will prevent you from leaving if that's what you wish to do, but I hope you'll consider staying, Miss Clark." He wanted her to stay, and not just because the company's president had asked him. Proving to her that the trip was one worth taking had become more important than he'd anticipated.

Before she reached the staircase, he called after her. "Miss Clark."

She stopped and looked over her shoulder.

"Please be careful when you come out on the sun deck." He looked down at her bare feet, and she followed his gaze. "Oftentimes the floor is wet and it's easy to slip. I wouldn't want you to get hurt."

She pivoted, raising her fingers in a mock salute. "Aye, aye, Captain."

ACKNOWLEDGMENTS

When I wrote Meet Me at Sunrise, I knew there was more to Afonso Cortez and his story. Afonso has had a hard time and when he meets Catarina, she's trying to rise from the lowest point in her life as well.

How could they not find happiness together? They're perfect for each other.

Of course, their journey is a hard one, and it wasn't less easy for me to write their story, but I'm glad I kept at it, and truly hope I've made them justice.

My thanks to Laura for being the greatest alpha reader and liking Afonso and Catarina from the beginning; to Michele for helping me straighten the story when the first version wasn't as good as it could be; to Lori, for her suggestions and for the interior formatting for the paperback book; and to Haley, for catching all the little things I always miss.

I'm glad for friends and professionals who help me turn my very rough drafts into the kind of stories my characters deserve. Thank you!

And thank you also to all the readers who've fallen in love with the Romanos!

THE AUTHOR

𝓛ucinda Whitney was born and raised in Portugal, where she received a Master's degree from the University of Minho in Braga, in Portuguese/English teaching.

She lives in northern Utah with her husband and four children. When she's not reading and writing, she can be found with a pair of knitting needles, or tending her herb garden.

She's the author of *Romano Family* series, of which Kiss Me At Midnight is the fifth book. She also authored *The Secret Life of Daydreams* and *One Small Chance*.

Please visit her website at lucindawhitney.com for more information and news.

www.ingramcontent.com/pod-product-compliance
Lightning Source LLC
Chambersburg PA
CBHW060540180626
46817CB00002B/665